NEW WRITING

VOLUME III

NEW WRITING
VOLUME III

Table of Contents

Introduction

1

To write anything you have to be able to feel everything. To write nothing you merely have to feel nothing. And you can write something and still write nothing. And that's what "content" is—that's who "content" makers are: inscribers of nothingness. The question then is: who *isn't* writing content? How can writing reclaim its status as poetry?

2

When I ride the subway in New York, and see people on their phones, heads tilted twenty-five degrees towards their feet, I feel like I'm living in a quiet little nightmare, where all the imagination and stubborn originality has fled from the human spirit and where we have all become nodes in an unfeeling web of information and power. The material, biological, and spiritual dimensions of human existence have become enmeshed with and drowned out by digital noise. On the subway, I watch advertisements streak by along the tunnel walls, and advertisements crop up on the screens of the phones around me, and my brain wants to sink into the pleasant/uncomfortable ooze of all this stimulus.

3

We reduce ourselves to the image of ourselves; believe in our own propaganda—this is what we use social media for: the printing of counterfeit selves; of a fake currency with which we purchase ontological stability. Who I am does not matter; what matters is the pseudo-self I project—the media platforms I've mastered. We do believe that we are more than sum our actions, our ethical commitments: we believe that we are the sum of our digital fictions.

4

Individuals die the way birds do: out of sight, almost invisibly. Our individuality dies without the pressure of the ethical, existential burdens; without the pressure of trying to be what we say we are. The Real is drying up. We externalize everything, internalize almost nothing. I notice that what people say they are—how they advertise their education, success, beliefs—is less and less indicative of who they are, or whom they will turn out to be; of depth and quality of soul.

5

Death is now an abstraction—death has been digitized. Floods, hurricanes, famines, shootings, bombings—these are abstrations we encounter on handheld screens. Media addiction is addiction to the concept that death is always elsewhere. We no longer experience death as a spiritual event: we experience it as information. Data.

6

Our culture excludes the poetic—the difficult; the figural; the manifold. We are addicted to easy representations. American culture is too easy.

7

If we could see the scars made by hyper-capitalism (mutating, algorithm-driven capitalism), if we could visualize the cognitive damage produced by our never ending exchange with product-placement — we would be sobered. We are all under pressure to brand ourselves; to monetize our image, our language.

8

Our superficial, socially mediated politics mirrors our superficial, socially mediated lives. Words and images are unreal, they do not reflect truth. A Twitter-President has merely grasped this behavioral logic. The more inwardness of self is displaced by the spectacle of self, the less it becomes possible to organize a virtuous resistance of living individuals.

9

I'm constantly forced to listen to my friends talk about a golden age of television, as if "great" television were anything less than eighth-rate Shakespeare or Tolstoy; watered-down philosophy; solidly acted melodrama.

10

Mistaking entertainment — which is another word for advertisement — for art, is a sin against the human spirit.

11

The decay of aesthetic thinking and feeling means a weakened capacity to recognize and engage with reality; to influence rather than be influenced.

12

Personally, I've always viewed aesthetics as the theory of magic-in-life, the unbundling of the ordinary into the extraordinary; as an existentialism: a tool for carving meaning and freedom out of meaningless automation; an ethics: an insistent demand for the creation and preservation and proper evaluation of the beautiful.

13

In New York, buildings, subway cars, skyscrapers, billboards all flash with some kind of advertising; so do phones, which we carry everywhere. Reality is de-aestheticized; drained not only of beauty, natural or created, but of the demand for beauty. Nobody rebels, nobody responds to this denuded environment; everyone carries on, as if nothing were the problem.

14

Living—really living—means chasing beauty from its hiding places—as if startling a flock of birds into the sky.

15

We can only hope that in mourning the selves we bury, we discover those selves anew.

MG
Serpent Club Press, General Editor
September 2017

Milk River Psalm

Michael Lavers

When the prolonged light of Alberta settles
the wild yarrow and the purple sage nibbling
at air, when the diffused light coarse as powdered
moths refracts the glimpsed-at destination
and the path, and, warmed in the imagination,
purpled granite greys the fraying feathers
of the goshawk—shiver, bite your tongue,
and let the white breath of the bison, invisible
all spring, all summer, hover, hoard the heat,
refract and multiply, moon-humid and nightblue,
what remains of the possible world, the veil
of elsewhere, here for a moment, then carried away.

The Blessing
Michael Lavers

So we put out the fires and started again.
We wheeled the books that were left
from the city of ashes to valleys where no one
would find us. We welcomed our grief.
We counted the past as the ruins of what was today.
The blue snow slept, and through the city
white hares seesawed over it on giant feet,
digging for anything green-edged or yellow-edged
that kept since spring. *There is no other life*
said the wind. *There is no other Earth*
said the Earth. The crows kept watch from
ordinary trees. For years it stayed like this.

I found myself very alone
by Zach Mahr

I was very alone in a foreign place. Me, the guy whose motivating ambition in life, up to this point, had always been to somehow maneuver himself into a comfortable room, one that had wi-fi and contained plenty of books, so that I could politely, quietly, but definitively shut a door in the face of the world. Where I found myself instead, I was able to recognize several chain stores, as well as basic foodstuff like cheeseburgers and ice cream, but otherwise I was totally disconnected from everything else. I shared only half a language with the family with whom I was staying, my past and future wife's family—we had come to get married.

We already married each other once, back home, we thought. That event had been as familiar to me as if I had done it a hundred times. There was a judge in my mother's backyard, between X and I, around whom my extended family stood as we exchanged vows; then everyone ate chicken parmigiana and ice cream cake. I had met X while I was in another, different foreign country (once again, where I had ended up not by my own choosing) and when we decided to marry, returning home was the practically inevitable way to start our life together. It was not until a month afterwards that I was informed that we were wrong. Our misunderstanding had something to do with bureaucracy, and with what was and what was not officially, literally, factually true. We waited two hours at the border to my wife's original country, which was reputedly a land of spectacular and fierce beauty, to which we had come for summer holidays, but the guard finally returned with our documents to tell me that they were unacceptable, that I was not, according to his employer's laws, my wife's husband, and that the only way I could join her, my 'wife,' on what had been our vacation, was if I intended to marry her while we were here.

My 'wife' was happy. She immediately began to plan, as soon as we arrived in her hometown, with the help of her sister, a second rehearsal dinner, a second, more elaborate and religious ceremony, and to invite all of her friends and her family members who had been unwilling or unable to travel to our USA wedding, for whom this occasion would be our real marriage. I, however, after all the hubbub and commotion entailed by wedding #1, had been longing for some peace. And we really found something, out in the rural countryside of this beautiful foreign place, an aestival paradise, where the the sun shone interminably, the rent was cheap, and I had brought plenty of books, with the intention of shutting the door. Only, each morning, at exactly coffee time, quickly in came what would have been my sister-in-law, Y, who was unable to wait until after breakfast: she wanted to to assist in the planning of what was, in my mind, a totally superfluous formality, but for her was a major milestone in her own life.

Y had her own husband, of course, who also had to sit around my breakfast table and discuss floral arrangements. He, too, was from a foreign country. Y had married him there in a wedding that was impromptu and unspectacular, presided over by a local civil servant, attended by strangers, and catered with inedible homemade local food. The few references that she made to her wedding were enough for me to understand that the day had not been ideal. Her husband, who to be fair was foreign, and although English-speaking communicated with her in another, third language that I didn't know, was almost barbarically unaware of how much obvious and traumatic pain he had caused his wife when he married her so indifferently. Not only did I allow Y to be part of the wedding my 'wife' and I might have shared exclusively between us, but I sucked up my selfish annoyance and distaste and I encouraged her to feel that it was partly hers, too.

The process took a long time, nearly a week. We would have coffee every morning, then breakfast, then tea, then a second coffee, which was followed by a second breakfast, while X and Y, mostly unassisted, negotiated between them how we would be definitively married. I would not have believed that two sisters, so otherwise close that they might be twins, could nonetheless diverge with such ferocity and at such a high volume, over the most minor details. Y would offer her opinion to X, who half of the time would reject it, so that Y would be forced to justify what she wanted. The vigor with which she would defend her position was, I began to suspect, a symptom of how insecure she was about wanting to co-opt her sister's wedding. Her certainty only got more and more defensive. Eventually, she had revealed not just her ideas, but a complete and total vision of how the wedding should be realized; a dream that she had obviously devoted years to nurturing, with a dedication and fatality that I found beautiful and, really, tragic. Its details got clearer and clearer as my 'wife' counterposed against it her own, different vision. But X would insist to me, at night, when I expressed concern, that her and her sister's squabbles were just their funny way of getting along, which would never full blow into any actual fight, which was true, until they fought about the cake.

5

My 'wife' was something of a health nut, for whom the idea of serving to all of our guests a mass of sugar, flour, and butter was horrific in the way that luring them somewhere dark in order to execute them, followed by burial in a mass grave, would be horrific. What would be far more sane and thoughtful, she felt, would be to serve everyone squares of dark chocolate and berries, instead. But Y's own wedding, she reminded us, had taken place in such a remote, poor village that she had had no choice: ingredients for a cake could not be bought, and to this day she regretted never having had a real wedding cake, one with tiers and marzipan, something that she told her sister she would also miss, in a year or two, once she got over her dumb health fad.

The woman who once was, and who would have been my wife knows this about me, that I have no authentic personal opinion about deserts. Y must have sensed my weakness. Together, they refused to decide themselves, and trapped me between them.

The next morning, I was up before coffeetime, before sunrise, because I had to walk along very rural roads for several hours, among flora and weeds totally unknown to me, until eventually I was guided by signs that I could not read back to the center of the town, where the only open shop is a jumbo supermarket. I had gone inside, to remind myself of exactly what a very, very familiar brand of packaged food looked like, when Y's husband touched me gently on the arm. I had no idea that he, too, sometimes came to the Ethnic Foods section.

We bought coffee from an automatic machine that we took to the front, outside, where the supermarket had placed shaded plastic patio chairs for its customers. We spoke English to one another, of course. For the entire morning, before we sat down to coffee, I had been allowing myself to dream. I had given myself permission to think about anything, and what I thought about with my freedom was where I would go, if I was allowed to go wherever I wanted. I had ended up constructing a whole highly developed picture in my head about what my life would be like there, one which I imagined to a hallucinatory level of detail that was so concrete and realistic that I felt like I needed to share it with someone; my 'wife' would only have misunderstood. But not only did Y's husband understand and sympathize, he knew all about the place I had made up in my head, since it turned out that this was the place where he had gotten married.

I boarded a ten-hour flight that evening. I had not packed headphones, or anything else, so I had to sleep rather than watch TV or read. This time, I dreamt about my own brother. By contrast, he insists that he will never get married, and he loves to travel to exotic places, but he still lives near home.

I had not imagined how cozy and remote my dream destination would be. It would have been impossible to reach, if I had not been told exactly how—via a series of buses that grew more infrequent and unreliable the further we got from the capital. I got increasingly less sure about where we were going, until I became unsure that we were going anywhere at all, when suddenly I arrived.

I should have known I would be expected. At the place that I would have described as a bus station, if it were located somewhere more familiar, all the locals stood waiting as the final bus arrived at my stop. I failed to make them understand that I was not him, whomever they would have been so happy to see, festively, forcibly steering him off the main plaza and down a random series of streets rather than me. They patted my head and smoothed down over my hair, though, talking in their other language, giving me many kisses. Eventually I was very solemnly, very considerately left alone in what was hinted was my own room; down the quietest street in town, we had paraded into the biggest house. Unpropped up and tired, I fell into a worn leather chaise longue, from which I could finally have a look at where life, which never fails to surprise me, had this time deposited me. This time there were shelves, floor to ceiling, full of books; of course, I could not read them—but they must have been interesting, and there were thousands of them. This was the kind of place I had always imagined where a man could very comfortably close himself up in. I dared myself to look, to check the door and make certain that this could actually be real, when I noticed the new, unworn wedding suit been placed on a clothing hook, hanging there. It disappeared, instantaneously, when the door very considerately opened, so a longish-faced, very deferential man could position a boutonnière within my reach before backing out, smiling, and then make it reappear once again as he closed the door.

Going the opposite direction from the one I was brought, the hallway outside led to a room that was just filled with religious stuff. But I continued into a much larger room, a chamber where everyone was already seated on long communal benches, quietly, looking behind them where I had abruptly, finally arrived.

The man with the longish face understood my mistake, and he led me back out of the worship hall, through the right door. Evidently the bluejeans and tee shirt that I had not changed out of were acceptable, since he didn't seem upset. If he was not so happy for me, I would have been able to explain why I wasn't dressed to get married, before he took me outside, in front of the church to meet my bride.

Y must have simultaneously imagined the same thing, in order to be there before me, wearing a gown, surrounded by half a dozen girls in dresses that matched hers. When I was ushered closer, though, and told Y how amazing it was—her face screwed into confusion and she called me by a name that wasn't mine.

The cafe reopened once the wedding was called off, so we could sit together, over cups of the local equivalent of coffee, to figure out exactly how hilarious our situation was. What seemed really disorienting and confusing turned out to be actually a very simple misunderstanding. It was much worse for her, though. She had actually been trying to get married, getting married had been her dream. Her fiance, to whose village she had travelled all the way from the far end of the world, somehow lost the will to show up. He didn't have a clear idea of what he wanted from life, she said. I felt awful for her.

By the time we understood one another, the entire congregation had begun to fill the cafe's other tables. They brought with them, on immense platters, what must have been prepared as our wedding feast, which they encouraged us to share with them, although I couldn't recognize anything as food and neither could she. They toasted to us and we, laughing, toasted them back, playing along, pretending to actually be the newlyweds that everyone had expected and hoped for. We agreed afterwards that we never could have had so much fun unless we actually got married.

This happened to us a while ago, now. So much has happened since, that it must have been a joke, or a dream, or another life.

A Response to "Melancholia"
Daniel Bossert

The titular planet "Melancholia," set on a destructive crash course for Earth, is undoubtedly—and perhaps too obviously—a grand symbol in von Trier's film. But it's not—just—a symbol for the apocalypse, for the end of the world, for Death. It's possible to make a good film, even a great one, without further specifying or narrowing that death-symbol down to a further level. But that's not what *Melancholia* does. For Death, when we immediately think of it, is so often this: the end of our existences. The fade-to-black of our lives. And perhaps something comes after…but that's outside the province of this film. Death is what ends our lives, here, now, perhaps forever. But (as the film shows us) we experience—either have experienced, or can experience—death in other forms, rather than just this immediate one that we have here, now, for ourselves.

One must become a parent, to the child that one—once—was…

The first time I watched the film, one of the elements that most caught my attention was the little boy, Leo, Claire's child and Justine's nephew. He's the only child in a film of adults, and—in a way—he seems unnecessary, a superfluous element, except insofar as he shows us that other characters are parents or aunts; that children (too) will die; etc. But, aside from that, as the two chapter titles tell us, this is Justine's film, fundamentally—and also, perhaps more subtly, Claire's film, as well. They are the two foremost characters, and it is their reactions to the events of the film—to the wedding, and to the approach of Melancholia—that define and center all that we see. The child provides a not-unimportant element, showing some sort of innocence and ingenuity, presenting some sort of childhood worry, and also calling forth some sort of extra caring (or lack thereof) on the part of the two main adults (or three, along with Claire's husband).

It was only the second time that I watched *Melancholia*, that this role of the boy came into my mind as a question, as a nagging element which almost doesn't need to be there, but which also does seems to be there, rather deliberately. And it was one of those impossible-to-trace leaps of logic that made me realize, as I looked at the child, how much he resembled Lars von Trier: the round face, the freckles, but above all the sandy-colored hair. How it seemed rather correct to think that this little boy—this actor—looked very possibly like how Lars von Trier would have looked as a child, himself. And then, suddenly, the entire film made sense: the film was not (just) a powerful investigation of our approaches to death, to depression, in the form of this planet named "Melancholia"— it was also a film about the death of childhood.

One must give to oneself the love, and the faith, that one needed—but didn't get—to carry one over that threshold of death...

Think of it this way: we all know death, even before we (one day) physically die. A symbolic death, yes, but one, for all that, not any less real—perhaps, in a way, just as important for our lives as the inevitable death that we also see and run from/towards. Childhood is this time in our lives when things seem so different, feel so different, from how they do—later—when we are adults, or even when we are adolescents. And they seem different, feel different, because—in a deeply powerfully way—they are different. When childhood ends—when that whole time of innocence, naivete, etc., ends—everything changes. And 'childhood' itself may be only an idealization, a wishfully created dream that writes over the much less rosy reality of our first years, but that doesn't make the sense—the symbol—the feeling—of 'childhood' any less real. Children, themselves, may not have a feeling of childhood; but we, as adults, without exception, undoubtedly know what it means to have been a child...and to be one no longer.

To correct the love that our parents failed to give us, by becoming—ourselves—parents, and trying to give that love to ourselves—as the children we once were—in the past...

Melancholia is a film about the death of childhood—and thus is a film for adults, those who remember (or who perhaps refuse to remember) that end of childhood, the moment when all those feelings of innocence and safety suddenly disappeared, died. And how, I think, that is what really makes the film as powerful, as it is, for those viewers whom it moves: because it does not just represent to us our approach to our deaths, now, but takes us back to that death that we once already experienced, when childhood—that time of happiness and worry-lessness—ended. Those moments when, suddenly, without totally understanding what is happening, your parents—who are usually so steady, so secure, so powerful, so indestructible—show worry, show fear, show terror, even— and you, yourself, cannot help but feel worry, fear, and terror, in turn. When, suddenly, all your sense of well-being—all the trust you have in your parents and the world they filter/ fill for you—ends, and you find yourself facing this looming impending SOMETHING, and you don't know what it is, or when it will come...You only know that something is happening, something is going to happen, that will change everything. And you are terrified, you fear it, like you've never feared anything before. Or at least this is how we feel, when we look back—as adults—on the first years of our lives, and the end of that sense of 'childhood' which we cannot help but carry with us.

And the world does end...'Childhood' is something that we all know, but only because we have lost it...Because the planet hit Earth, and we—as children—died...

Late in the film, after all the characters (slowly) realize that the planet is going to hit Earth, and they are all going to die...what do they do? The father kills himself. The mother grabs her son, and runs around frantically, all over their estate, clutching him to her chest, trying in vain to find a safe place, but only serving to pass her agitation and horror onto her son. And what does Justine, her sister, the little boy's aunt—whom he calls throughout the film Auntie Steelbreaker—do? She, of all of them, is the only one who seemingly can handle the fact of Melancholia, can face up to the fact of their impending death. And this, I think, is where von Trier's evocation of the death of childhood becomes extremely personal. And also where it becomes about art, as much as it is about life. For how does Justine, at the end of the film, interact with the little boy, as his parents are losing control and cannot bear— themselves—what is going to happen? She calms him down, she reassures him that everything is going to be okay. She—

the one who, to him, can do anything, who can even break steel—has the idea that they will build a magic tent, where they won't get hurt. Because, as she explains, nothing can hurt them if they're in the magic tent. And it doesn't matter— to the little boy—that this magic tent is only a few long sticks leaning against each other, to form a sparse, meager-looking tepee. What matters—and what will matter, even after Melancholia hits the earth and kills them all—is that he believes what his Aunt tells him: that they will all be safe, inside that magic tent. He listens to her, when she tells him to close his eyes. And there's this look of calm that comes onto his face, with his eyes closed…because he trusts his aunt, and because he believes what she says, believes that magic can— in fact—protect and save them. That a few bare sticks put together—that the things that come into your head when you close your eyes—that imagination—that art—has a power, to stop even what feels like—what is—the end of the world…

And imagination, and art, does not save you…But—still— perhaps in spite of himself, perhaps because it was (and always will be) his last unfulfilled hope, and his final unrealized salvation, Lars von Trier, that frightened, sandy-haired little body, still believes in art…

In the last scene of the film, as Justine, Leo, and Claire sit together inside the magic tent, Justine tells them all to take each other's hands…And she tells them to close their eyes… And the little boy does this, and—his eyes closed, one of his hands being held by his beloved aunt, and one of them being held by his mother—he has this look of peace (and of trust) on his face…But Claire, his mother, can't keep her eyes closed…And she can't keep the fear, and the terror, from

15

surging through her body...She is crying, and shaking, and grimacing, as each second Melancholia gets closer and closer, and she watches it with her eyes...Justine, on the other side, also has her eyes open, but she is just looking at her nephew, and looking at her sister, and calmly—if tensely—taking it all in...Trying to convey some sort of steadiness—perhaps some sort of affection, some sort of message—to her sister, but failing to do so, as Claire is shut off from everything but her own fear...And then, in the very last shot of the film, there's 'Melancholia', this large white circle, growing and growing, almost filling the entire background of the scene...And then, in the foreground, down at the bottom of the screen, almost dwarfed by the approaching white mass, are the dark outlines of two figures—two women—inside a tent made of sticks... And they are holding each others' hands...But then, a single moment before Melancholia hits the Earth, and plows up the ground underneath them, and the screen flashes suddenly to black, in one of the most blunt and final endings to any film ever...In the last moment where we can still see these figures, Claire—so overcome with it all, unable to handle what is a second away from happening—pulls her hands out from Justine's, and also out from her son's, and clutches her head in her hands, shaking uncontrollably...In that last moment, right before the final cut to black, Justine is still holding the little boy's hand, and she is—now—the only one able to do so...

And yet, even through that death, through that ending, his trust—his belief—in magic stays with him...And will always stay with him...Even as he (perhaps) grows up, and cannot help but try to create—to stay true—to that magic, himself... The magic of art and imagination...The magic of film...

If Lars von Trier represents himself/his story by the little boy in the film, then he also represents himself by Justine...By the artist...Justine, the one who is famed for her incomparable ability to find the catchphrase, to find the right words and to create the perfect product...But also—just as importantly, if not moreso—she is the one who, in the truest sense, is a parent...In that very last shot, Claire—in a way—ceases to be a parent...The little boy is still her son, but—in that moment, when she pulls her hands out from his, in order to clutch (in agony) her own head—she is not his parent...She is just a person, an individual, who is going to die, and knows it, and is utterly terrified by it...In that last shot, she is not thinking about her son, because she can't...And that's not to fault her, in a way, because she IS—herself—her life and her entire existence—going to die...And that IS terrifying...And who wouldn't understand—wouldn't sympathize—with the irresistible urge to clutch our heads in our hands, when our world is literally falling apart?...But, on the other side of that small tent, constructed simply of sticks, is Justine, who looks around at her nephew and her sister, who tries to calm them each down, and who—in the last shot—is still holding her nephew's hand...Who holds his hand—his small child's hand—until the very end...And that, I think, is what Lars von Trier sees in a parent...As someone who not only thinks of another, and who not only places a child—his wants, his needs—before her own, but who does that even in the worst of times, even in the moment when the world—literally—is ending...Claire, in that last moment, is overwhelmed by Death, but Death as HER death, as the Death of HER existence...In that last moment, she is overwhelmed by herself, by the reality of her own body, and of her own impending annihilation...Justine, until the very end, remains aware of others, of their bodies, of their wants and needs...And even, in a deep way, she remains aware of their deaths—of what death is/will be, for them, and not (just) what it will be, for herself...Melancholia, in those last moments, is not just a symbol of her own death, so close and imminent...But also—also—it is a symbol of the death of others, of other individuals, besides oneself...A symbol of the end of their lives...Of the end of their existences...It's the end of the life of someone else, someone whom you care about so much, that—in a way—you are able—able and willing—to see beyond your own death, and to see their death, the death of themselves, as well...

And how that last second rupture of the connection between the little boy and his mother—and earlier, too, when his father commits suicide—is perhaps the most essential part of the death of childhood...

That may very well be an idealization of parenthood, just as what I described earlier is an idealization of childhood and its end...And yet: why should that make it any less powerful, any less valuable, or any less true?...Isn't that what a parent—a true parent—does, and would do, at the very end of the world?...To see another's death, to see Death as something that will happen to others, just as much as it is something—a horrible something—that will happen to you, yourself?

This second symbolization of "Melancholia"—as the death of another—though, was not one that came to me at the same time as the first symbolization...But that, I think, says more about me, and where I was, than about the film...Because, in a way, I think that the film shows—if not argues—that to be able to represent the death of childhood, one must become (truly) a parent...And vice versa...That one of these movements cannot be completed, in art—and perhaps in life—without the other...As if it is death—this multi-varied symbol of Death—that connects childhood and parenthood, together...As if, even though a parent cannot stop the end of the world, cannot stop either themselves—or their children— from dying, a parent, still, in some way, eases that transition... Makes the loss of childhood less catastrophic...Or maybe just gives to a child something—trust, a belief in magic, a faith in art—that will allow them to deal with and to face, what comes after...

Perhaps only in order for them to become parents, and to pass that trust, that belief, that faith (that illusion?) onto their own children...

And I think Lars von Trier is also saying: that one does not need to have a child, oneself, to be a parent...How one can be a parent to—perhaps—anyone, so long as you love them enough, to place their death (in some sense) before your own...And thus, also, to place their life, before your own... Because the death of childhood is a horrible moment, that— unfortunately—we all must go through, in order to become adults...But maybe that's okay—maybe that's not so bad—if we still have something, whether it's an impulse toward art, or the love given to us by another, to carry us through it... To carry us through, even what may turn out to be the end of the world...

Response to the Film "Star Garden" by Stan Brakhage

Anthony Delluva

To watch light pass through vacant rooms; rooms already gone, rooms where we are not—Brakhage offers us this glimpse into these rooms of light and memory. I think of mental flashes of parts of my-Home; parts of my-Self. The title *Star Garden* suggests a meteor that has fallen, a vast crater...But a meteor that has carried with it life instead of death; it is in this crater where Brakhage's family is left to themselves to dance with light and shadow, sun and moon. What mental state is star garden: sublimated distance.

A fecund verdure and the jewel glimmer of Suns; Brakhage takes us to the suspended country of outer-space. Lunch and Dinner. A jar of Jam; that brilliant red space-debris. An incredible warmth and tenderness; that rare and profound moment of the family synergizing; moments I see in flashes, somehow captured—re-ified! This is the paradox of the flux of film; the unrepeatably moving and fluid can be played again. What are the colorized, filtered/inverted frames at the beginning of *Star Garden*? A before time? Images...and then a spider! To weave together! This spider-sun is a weaving of light over the course of a day. This star garden is an enlivened enlightened somnambulism. A re-turn to the profundity of our givens through careful observation; and the subsequent launching into space; star garden is a science fiction of our everydayness.

Before Genesis
Claire Åkebrand

darkness filled
with the sound of a rustling sea
she tried not to wonder
where the dark had
come from
               waves slowing
dreams of carnations
sunrise a book on
the nightstand and
lines of laundry in the sun
         someone singing
                  she woke with a song's
taste on her tongue
tried to hum it but couldn't
remember the tune half-asleep
she reeled to the window

Geode
Claire Åkebrand

Break open
the night
like a rock,
eons
in the making,
to find:

the crystals
of dew on asters.

Pretend there were
such a thing:
June
morning.

Pile / of Stone
Leonard Zawadski

and we rest upon the Earth / beneath
a cloudless sky / considering the place within

this universe we hold / not unlike: a flower /
not unlike: a stone—or, single blade

of grass // and we sing a solemn melody / on
Harmony / in a golden field / away

from the bustling City // and we seek
to discover ourselves / amongst the stars and,

within the bright-light of day, / as
a Sedge Wren might / singing: itself, upon

the bare-branch of autumn // and we forsake
all Capital's entreaty—who speaks

through the teeming City / not spending, (simply)
being Time // and follow each moment

with a wholehearted breath / each note
rings-out immaculate sound / as tho from bells

of an unheralded monastery // and we found an
alternative pathway to Presence / mattering

wholly in motion,
at last. ///

[A Solitary Chore]
Leonard Zawadski

a solitary chore, becomes a prac-
tice of mindful-ness, the moment one accepts
an avenue, its: wealth of house, rich
delineal of Autumn-leaf, and opulent emp-
ti-ness—for what it is

               a rivulation, then
ensues, turning the Body whole again
 to the mind—engulphs the individual; it sit-
uates (in no uncertain terms) at where
exactly all can be;   re-stratifies to one-
ness, even-ing ev'rything out

                so, one stands
enraptured—this way: eyes like beads
of boundless satiety, an awed half-smile,
completely without thought

              and taken, now
will walk (at once)

        to where-ever
        one must be.

Peace Lily
Leonard Zawadski

you seem, dare i say it, even happy
in our red ceramic nest—one leaf twirling

as though in dance, and out upon the room
/ a main flower open, as though an-

ticipating an embrace—bearing its
product of centuries (innumerable), quite

a display! 'what shape *is* that?' // imagining
you in the still of an absent house,

beside a sleeping dog, comfortable
, and proud—such a sublime tenderness,

passing the hours // i begin to weep…(un-
ashamedly) for what quietude you

represent, after all—and then, i breathe a deep breath, recompose myself at

a table of tea, settle down // oh, strings of
an unbearable lament! how true it

is that: yesterday is gone—Time,
vanishing, /ter/s us asunder; bathes us wi-

th-in Its terrible ardor; ventures, without
hesitation / (succeeds), in passing!

Out of Nothing
Leonard Zawadski

it is quiet, again—a room we
inhabit, sit within, and upon / its golden

floor-boards: so untouched /
lay these piano keys, of our internal sound //

and so, Sunday becomes, *this* way—as we…
   inhale…exhale…the void; ex-

   amine / a silent petal—silk upon
an endless sky; exist as space; exhibit love;

extend into an ocean: Temporality / ourselves
   one self, our hands one hand, and

   heart abeat in unison, with-what
but an *incorruptible singularity* / thus, parity

envelops us (continues to, that is) as *What
   Is* // our separation falls away, di-

stance (in fact) disappears, and we breathe //
   "what remains?" (other than / an

   eternal weightlessness?) "A technicality, a
   vision: two translucent pyramids,

   connected base to base (seamlessly)
then, internally baseless & rotating / about its

point-to-point axis / at forty-five° from Xs, Ys
and Zs /…it is *Life Force*—at ev'ry

moment being felt—a /tir/; a tooth; /'tambər/
of a voice—each and ev'ry vacillation

of Itself-Known, -Not-Known, and
-Not-Knowable / the pathway between home

and wilderness; birth and death; each breath;
the quiet of this room" // and we open

our eyes, and embrace one another,
(tenderly), with joy ///

One Morning
Leonard Zawadski

nestled within th

e calm aire of a solitary medit

ation / breath li

ke an unusually p

roud and profound wandering / s

tanding beside th

e river as it flo

ws from the mountainside / sitt

ing upon the floo

r of a room richl

y lit and warm as a noon of lat

e springtime / no

thought of a flo

wer blooming / nor buds as they

blossom / at mid

night an orchard
/ apples hung like knowledgeabl
e orbs of existen

ce / golden inter
ior / smooth carpet of Earth /
amongst the great

One not One to b
reathe / an ocean of Emptiness
/ here is the Whe

rewithal / here i
s the Utmost and Epitome / the
Very Central and

Singular of *It All*
1 / the Interconnectedness and
} Inter }penetration
  of Being non Bein
g / *not unlike how a kettle res*
  ts upon the table

.

31

Summer in the Library
Honor Devi Thapa

The books in the fiction section had already been shelved twice and Adrienne was bored. It was mid-July and even though the air conditioner had been broken for almost a week and nobody came into the library, management refused to close. Normally Adrienne didn't mind reading at work on a quiet day, but the humid air made her feel sleepy and romantic. After reading countless adventures in books, she longed for something to happen in her own life. She looked around. The library was small, and it didn't take long for her to find Alex sitting on the floor, reading Rilke.

"It's so hot," she said.

"Yeah." Alex didn't look at her.

"I'm tired of reading. Let's play a game."

"Like what?" Alex turned a page placidly.

"The question game."

"Sounds deceptively simple." He smiled.

"It is." Adrienne sat beside him on the floor. "I ask you any question I want and you have to answer."

"I see. A game of your own invention."

"You get to ask a question, too."

Alex flipped through the rest of the book.

"Alright."

"Great. You go first."

Alex thought for a moment.

"No. You go first. I can't think of anything."

"Alright, fine. Let me think." Adrienne scanned the shelves. "What were you like as a kid?"

"Oh. I was pretty shy, I guess."

"Yeah? Me too."

"Really—I can't imagine you being shy."

"Everyone says that. But I was. I didn't talk to anyone except my mom."

"You didn't talk to your dad?"

"My dad wasn't around," she said quietly.

"Oh. Sorry."

"You're blushing," she said.

"I know." Alex covered his face with his hands.

"It's cute." Adrienne let her hand fall near his leg. "Anyway, it's your turn."

"How long have you worked at the library?" He smiled.

Adrienne stared blankly at him.

"I'm not even answering that. That might be the most underwhelming question ever asked in the history of the Question Game."

He laughed.

"Have my question asking capabilities been revoked?"

"Yes. As a matter of fact, they have." Her hair skimmed her burnt shoulders. "I get to ask as many questions as I want until you can think of a question worth asking."

"Do you make up the rules as you go along?"

"Maybe."

"I guess that's fair."

"Let's see. What are your biggest pet peeves?"

"Oh, hm." Alex scratched his ear. "Bad drivers."

"That's everyone's pet peeve!"

"Is it? I guess you're right."

"Think of something else."

"I dunno."

"I'm going to have to up the ante here."

"Yeah?"

"Yeah."

"Okay. Hold on." Alex closed his eyes. "I'm ready."

"Good. Why did your last relationship end?"

"Distance."

"How many girls have you said 'I love you' to?"

"Five."

"How many times did you mean it?"

"Two."

"Interesting."

"Keep 'em coming."

"It's fun, right?"

"Yeah."

"Let's see…When was the last time you cried?"

"When my grampa died."

"Where's the craziest place you've had sex?"

Alex smiled.

"In a tree."

"What?"

"Yeah."

"Really?"

"Yes," he laughed.

"I don't believe you. That's kind of amazing."

Alex blushed.

"How the fuck did you manage that?"

"My ex used to babysit these kids. They were out of town one weekend, and they had a treehouse…"

"Oh. Well that explains it."

"What about you?"

"What?"

"What's your craziest place?"

"Not a little kid's treehouse," she said. Alex laughed.

"Okay. So where was it then?"

"It's subjective, really."

"Come on," Alex said. "I answered all your questions."

"No, really. There are a few."

"Well?"

"Okay," she sighed. "There's the woods. And a fire escape. And one time at work—"

"Work?"

"Yeah."

"Here?"

"No," she laughed.

"Well then where? How? Spill."

Adrienne smiled.

"I had a key."

Alex smiled. He paused for a moment.

"I thought of a question." He leaned in toward her.

"Yeah?"

She looked at him, then looked down.

"Yeah."

He was a few inches away from her face.

"Okay."

Adrienne felt her heart beat faster.

"What turns you on?" Alex whispered.

"Everything," she said. He leaned in—

She stopped herself. Alex didn't notice her staring at him from across the room. Adrienne watched him as he read his book. She cleared her throat.

"Hey," she said. "What are you reading?"

Ohio September Ago
Lis Fertig

Sharp day Brooklyn early June
same as how Ohio September ago
getting into compact car or just the fact of your Volvo
dash all beach glass,
static and cigs, headphones asnarl,
felt pilling and postnasal chords,
so I'm
what's the word for
having a memory that isn't yours?

I offer
clean crunching into glass
like I've always wanted
backseat sky a
Bombay sapphire:
That is—dry martini in the hand
of the author as a thin blade of glass
slid between the panes
of what I said and meant,
forgetting I'm drunk, no,
a half galaxy on tip of tongue,
had it in shower now it's gone or
to name a few more—
the recent green truck, Easter dress, night falling on the
desert,
or here's uneasy one
all the times I've almost come
all those rides too soon for gin

safe inside my appetite
but where you might drive us
to the travesty of ice cream.

You all get extra butter
I half a cup of sky
ask me why and I'm
ok thanks but
isn't anyone caring
for my sharp definition
Where's the pain in precision
Could I wait in the car?

Two Dreams

Lis Fertig

read that story twice last night
but missed what it was about
except that a   scorpion crawled
inside the woman's mouth
and maybe she was dreaming
it's getting harder and harder
to tell now and anyhow I'll suffer
and bask just as deep on both sides
only difference I can see is here's
where's my bank account and
even that has ghost-like aspects

versus   [1] the   train   on stilts
across that glacial bay of which
we even took many photos, Ben and I,
which I burn to share with everyone,
a simple answer   provided by the
arrangement of water and trees
that cools   [2] the ringing sadness
of the best forever love
who   once again   could not survive
the trip to the bank
or couldn't   wait   unaltered

which reminds me of forever's
great escapes: a   funny   way
of shimmering out just when
you're banking on him so could it be

something like the way I was
at that gas station when I was fourteen—
but it's not what you think
just a   strawberry mouthfeel—
is it still mine?
do I grit my teeth when I pet the cat?
I could learn to bring it with me,
just need   time

The Swimming Lesson
Lis Fertig

A woman will be an example of an animal
will wild dim experience
                 if serious or blind
that is settle into the cast
                 if sand or wax
or over armature enormously fit
                 not flush or fettered
                 of fault or murder

as the idea of an apartment
is not a window or the floor
                 or wash of shouting tides
                 or place to pour a guilty drink
is from down in the street a bloodlight
                 (the boy undressing shadow)
is from inside maybe just not rain

as concrete drinks blood black
if dimming garage lamp
says so is merlot
while every bottlegreen shard just goes
oh no
and nothing so much as,
this hasn't happened yet, has it?
or *je refuse*

bottom of the ocean
a stooping blue conclusion

blood blood blood blood
                blood unbounded!

The swimming lesson will be a literature of drowning
               of fluid inclusion
one tidal wave of spilled boys' mothers
            if brunt of uncles
            who brought us McDonald's
will wash us down,
consume and guide us back out and around.

Chaos and Form: The Creation of Poetry
Michael Lavers

> *Whether it is an organized universe or chaos huddled together,*
> *it is still a universe.*   *—Marcus Aurelius*

All poems have form. We open up a book and notice poem-esque shapes. We hear somebody reading sounds more patterned than colloquial speech, more metrical, more alliterative, more sonically textured, or more rhetorical. Out of the swirling mist of "daily life" a poem appears, a little boat. We hop on board, it ferries us across the eddy of a minute, maybe two. We disembark, and it recedes again. To do this, it must be of a different substance than the elements around it. Or rather, it must rearrange those elements—space, sound, matter, time—into something that those elements are not, something more permanent and sure.

1

In the beginning there was only water. Land or sky or time or space had not appeared yet, only churning turbulence without design or end. This is our species' favorite metaphor for whatever predates substance and solidity and shape, whatever quantum foam there was before the universe appeared. First chaos, or the "total arsenal of entropy," as Ovid calls it and as Ted Hughes translates (3); then Earth somehow, and then an atmosphere, and then this cup of tea exhaling next to me, stray atoms scattered through the universe and now corralled together in this little rim.

The metaphor is elegant and simple, and yet therefore self-consuming, since its very aptness automatically negates the image of disorder it's meant to evoke. What drop of ink, or smear of paint, or twitch of vocal cord would not seem, in its very formedness, a kind of anti-chaos? The "total arsenal of entropy" cannot really exist, we think, if sounds can be combined to make that phrase, and then to make that phrase last.

Above the entrance to Plato's academy was carved the motto "Let no one ignorant of geometry enter here," establishing knowledge of mathematical form as a precondition for any other kind of learning. Einstein, as if only elaborating on this point, proved spacetime is not nothing, but a thing itself, a measurable, formal substance that flows out of objects, and which bends and folds and caves. We might not ever know what nothingness or total chaos looks like since the existence of that observation would be proof against it. There is nothing that is not something, no chaos—at least in this dimension—without form.

Milton makes much of this paradox in *Paradise Lost*, nullifying chaos slightly by describing it in strict blank verse: "Illimitable Ocean without bound, / Without dimension, where length, breadth, & highth, / And time and place are lost" (2.892-894). What vexes Milton's Satan is what vexes all of us, and younger poets are especially embarrassed to admit that they aren't "self-begot, self-rais'd" (5.860). They're angry when they're told poetic forms predate them, and that a sonnet, for example, has strict rules to which they must conform.

So they rebel. Or try to, anyway. But those who try because they think too many structures will inhibit creativity only replace the tyranny of conventional forms with the tyranny of unconventional ones. Sometimes the change can lead to the sublime, but sometimes we look back and see the steps of heaven have been swapped for burning marl.

2

When my children were born, we lived near the mountains. The five miles of air between our house and Thurston Peak (9706 ft.) seemed more like one or two in spring when honey-colored sagebrush was in bloom. The distance seemed to double or quadruple when the white-on-white refractions of the winter light on snow appeared to amplify the space between. These shifts in distance weren't just seasonal; each day had its advancements and retreats. I often thought of Wordsworth, underneath that cliff, rowing his little boat,

> *When from behind that craggy Steep, till then*
> *The bound of the horizon, a huge Cliff,*
> *As if with voluntary power instinct,*
> *Uprear'd its head. I struck, and struck again*
> *And, growing still in stature, the huge Cliff*
> *Rose up between me and the stars, and still,*
> *With measur'd motion, like a living thing,*
> *Strode after me. (1.405-412)*

My children, though, never noticed the mountain. Even though they were both born right next to it, they didn't seem to see it for their whole first year. I'd push their stroller through the neighborhood and feel the mountain follow us, its ring of mist like hot breath at my neck. I'd turn and face it, and could feel the mountain flinch. But when I tried to point it out to them I'd see their gaze land either on the row of houses under it, or on the wedge of daymoon hanging overhead. I thought about those *Magic Eye* illusions where, if you look *through* the page, *inside* the chaos, then distinct 3-D shapes start to emerge: a T-rex, or a castle, or a pod of floral-printed dolphins caught mid-leap above a rippling sea. What I thought was a very solid outline demarcating "craggy rock" as foreground and "blue sky" as background was, in fact, a difference that an infant needs about a year to master.

To really see a poem takes equal time and effort. Sometimes you have to burry content in a mess of marginalia before the underlying forms, the poem's "measured motion," swim into focus: syntax, vowel sounds, word length, caesuras, assonance, stress. We notice, in those lines by Wordsworth, how the s sounds mingle with the c's to coax out of the page the slosh of water and the scoop of oar. We notice how repeated words and phrases boost the passage's momentum. We notice how enjambment emphasizes both the bulk of *Lake*, *Boat*, *Swan*, and *Cliff*, and that they too, despite their heft and speed, are trapped inside the amber light of time, in *then*, *again*, and *still*. The poem is recreating one of those events in life that is both isolated and recurring, both sped-up and stuck. We notice no two lines are metrically identical, and most of them are metrically irregular. We notice that the final sentence walks us through a little labyrinth of subordination, as if tripping itself, or looking back over its shoulder, until the final startle of "strode after me," the person who we thought of as the agent and the focal point of the entire scene now buried in a pile of parentheticals.

Content can alert us to the existence of experiences that are not ours. And this is no small thing. But only form can make us feel what little Wordsworth felt: small, lost, hunted, crushed.

No doubt the content of the poem has primed me to imbue its formal architecture with these tinges of the ominous. No doubt a different poem could copy all these forms to talk about the sunlight in the daffodils, for instance, and no doubt we'd say how perfectly these self-same structures caught that scene's emotions and its smells. Writing of the celebrated lines of Pope which argue that "the sound must seem an echo to the sense," Dr. Johnson cautions us against expecting a mimesis of form and content:

> This notion of representative metre, and the desire of discovering frequent adaptations of the sound to the sense, have produced, in my opinion, many wild conceits and imaginary beauties…there is supposed to be some relation between a soft line and soft couch, or between hard syllables and hard fortune… Beauties of this kind are commonly fancied, and, when real, are technical and nugatory, not to be rejected and not to be solicited. (741)

"The mind," as he says, "often governs the ear" (741), and we would be bad readers if we imposed these kind of resemblances where they don't exist. They usually don't exist. What makes something a poem isn't that its forms are mimetic of its content, but that the forms are its content. Everything from phonemes to spondees to sentence variation and narrative patterns. Even metaphor, something thought of as primarily imagistic, is driven by an impulse that is formal: this shape is like that, this smell is like that. Metaphor is the making of parallels, the making of order, the reduction of chaos. A poem is nothing but an accumulation of these forms, of structures that fall like layers of silt into a final sediment, and give the poem its weight and gravity, its craggy north face and its sunny south. They give ideas that grow from them a flavor and a texture that cannot survive paraphrase, and which are untranslatable.

3

On September 4 1962, Anna Akhmatova and Robert Frost met for lunch at a large dacha some fifty miles outside Leningrad. She was 73 years old, and Frost was 88. He declined to recite any of his own verse, but asked to hear something by her, and she obliged. In a recording made in Cambridge in 1965, her manner of reading is unhurried, her voice hushed slightly by age, but careful to accentuate the rhythmic, crescendo-like power of her verse. Frost knew no Russian, but, according to F.D. Reeve who accompanied Frost on his journey, he was "moved by the poet's voice," and praised the only thing he could: "It's very musical. You can hear the music in it. It's very good" (107).

We don't generally read or listen to poetry in languages that we don't know, but this is not to say such poetry can't move us. Eliot wrote that "genuine poetry can communicate before it is understood," claiming that even those of us who can't understand Italian can be moved by Dante, can feel the music of the original (200). Without access to the content of the poem, we are left only with form, with language as an incantation. Its real power, as an artifact of sound, lies somewhere beyond meaning, in forms that are communicable outside of semantics; that's what makes it a poem. Pater, most famously, claims that although we can "distinguish between the matter and the form" of a poem, "the ideal types of poetry are those in which this distinction is reduced to its minimum" (107-108), poems in which form and content "present one single effect" (109).

When Reeve says Frost was "moved" by the poem, this can be understood not just figuratively, but literally and physically. To read a poem is to have your body moved around by another body, the way a tuning fork can make a resonant guitar string start to vibrate from afar. Hearing a poem is an experience of amplitude and frequency, of volume, pitch, and speed, of resonances and echoes of those sounds inside the room, inside the objects in the room, including you, the listener, whose body becomes part of the poem's acoustic signature. Shelley begins his "Defense of Poetry" with this claim:

> Man is an instrument over which a series of external and internal impressions are driven, like the alternations of an ever-changing wind over an Æolian lyre, which move it by their motion to ever-changing melody. But there is a principle within the human being, and perhaps within all sentient beings, which acts otherwise than in the lyre, and produces not melody alone, but harmony, by an internal adjustment of the sounds or motions thus excited to the impressions which excite them. (511)

This is why raves exist. This is what dancing is. The same thing happens when a wineglass smashes if you sing to it just right. Anyone who's read a poem and felt their knees buckle, their skin shiver, their heart waver and break knows how this works. I have had this experience listening to recitations of Dante's Italian, although I couldn't understand a single word. The best poems have been tuned to emit just those patterns of sound that echo in us and against us. Poems that make our hair flicker and buzz.

I sometimes wonder, therefore, if the pathetic fallacy is entirely fallacious, if the metaphor "Big Bang" is meant to describe the noise of the creation or creation's cause. In Greek mythology, Linus was the music teacher of Orpheus and Hercules, and when he died his mourners' dirge was so loud that it permanently altered space. In the first Duino elegy (trans. Edward Snow), Rilke describes their lamentation as "vibrations—/ which for us now are rapture and solace and help" (9). Our cries might not tear space, or make the willows tremble or the spruces shake, but they can break glass. And more importantly, they offer solace. They can do this since— the cliché must be allowed—they resonate. The vibrations of a poem, if you allow them to, will shake you. They will stir the water in your inner ear, and chime that trio of small bones. Your body is the poem's sonorous world, its medium and its message, its matter and its energy. Inside of you some chaos finds its form. The poem moves, a "single wave," as Rilke says, "whose gradual sea I am" (*The Poetry of Rilke* 405).

4

Thou, paw-paw-paw; thou, glurd; thou, spotted
    Glurd; thou, whitestap, lurching through
The high-grown brush; thou, pliant-footed,
    Implex; thou, awagabu. (43)

So begins John Hollander's poem "Adam's Task." There are four more stanzas like this, but in theory there's material for maybe millions more: with just a few base elements inside a strand of DNA there is no limit to the number of potential permutations, or the number of words we could dream up to name those permutations. So too, in the realm of poetry whole menageries of species and sub-species exist: sonnets, villanelles, epigrams, elegies, odes, sestinas, heroic couplets, blank verse, ballads, dramatic monologues, terza rima, ottova rima, vers libre, eclogues, sapphics, accentual verse, Spenserian stanzas, rondeaux, and limericks. Other islands have their own endemic species, some of which—the pantoum, haiku, ghazal—have migrated and interbred with native species, while countless others—the sijo, muwaššaḥ, buraanbur—have yet to make it to our shores.

Each of these forms is shaped, through centuries of environmental pressures or habits of breeding, to crack open certain thoughts, or pollinate a certain species of experience. The ballad, crammed with different kinds of repetition (not just stanza shape and tight-knit rhymes, but a refrain, and broad recurrences of character and plot) is poised to re-enact the reoccurring and inevitable: shipwrecks, love affairs, battles, dreams. Sestinas, by comparison, have evolved a different form of repetition: end-words rotate inside fixed stanzas, but in a pattern that seems almost designed to be forgotten, stretched by distances that dim the echo. The pleasure of predictability is lost, but in its place we get the pleasure of surprise by seeing how inventively the author can reuse the same ingredients. In superb sestinas, you might not notice the constraint at first, but soon you'd start to feel it, a mild, not-entirely-unpleasant claustrophobia, like spending an entire morning at your favorite window, watching the same few blue jays come and go.

These aptitudes are not unique or absolute. The woodpecker finch has learned to compensate for its short tongue by using twigs and sticks as tools to fish out bugs from trees. Sonnets can parrot the narrative propulsion of ballads, and ballads can mimic the meditations of a sonnet. Even among organisms of the same species, enormous variety exists; as Robert Haas writes, "no two sonnets...have the same form" (65), despite the fact that for the first few centuries of the sonnet form, their subject matter rarely strayed from love and its attendant desolations. It wasn't that the authors continued to uncover new thematic ground that kept them going: it was the thrill of getting at the same old story with a different strain of rhyme or strut of rhythm, some fresh plumage that could make love seem brand new each time. The twentieth-century architect Louis Kahn puts it this way: "The essential thing, you see, is that a chapel is a personal ritual, and that it is not a set ritual, and it is from this that you get the form" (44). In order to achieve maximum power and resonance, a sonnet too—or any poem written in an inherited form—must be both personal—that is to say, unique—and ritualistic. It must conform to certain traditional patterns, but in its own way. Each generation seems prone to fetishize the new, the different, the original, and the "organic," over the traditional, the familiar, and the artificial. But Northrop Frye observes that,

> critics who stress the imitation of nature usually
> have a strong respect for tradition...The parents of
> a new baby are proud of its novelty; they may even
> speak of it as unique; but the source of their pride
> is the fact that it is a recognizable human being, and
> conforms to a prescribed convention...In literature
> as in life the unconventionally new is a monstrosity.
> (43)

All good poems are conventionally new. The gene pool of the cannon is sustained by the anti-canonical flowing into it. Immutability emerges from mutation.

Although poetic forms are made with ink and paper, or syllables and soundwaves, they are products of the human animal, and are born and live and die inside our bones and brains. It's true, as Frye says, that "the impulse to give a literary shape to something can only come from previous contact with literature" (42). Upon getting the news of the death of a friend, we do not burst spontaneously into a pastoral elegy—we weep. Nor do we speak, when in love, as Romeo and Juliet, in intertwined and highly-structured sonnets. Poetic forms, in other words, are not spontaneous secretions. But neither are birds' nests. And like a nest, a poem is the product of a mouth, woven out of small pieces of the world, packed tight with the delight and detritus of life. They're both the result of some strange alchemy of deliberation and instinct, work and whim, artifice and inner pain that only artifice can heal.

My students sometimes make a version of this argument by petitioning my strict "no electronics in the classroom" policy by saying that their laptop or tablet is a "prosthetic extension" of their brain. And they might be right. But if laptops are prosthetic, then so is a sonnet. So is a book. So are libraries. All of these forms are so intimately are part of us that to live a life without them would feel like an amputation. Take away sestinas and it might feel like missing only three small toes; but blank verse would be the legs and a lung. And sonnets both the heart and head.

If all we asked our art to do was hold a mirror up to nature, the best art would be the biggest, the painting or novel that took up as much time and space in nature as nature itself, one of Borges's libraries or labyrinths. According to Aristotle, such a work of art wouldn't be beautiful: animals and poems, he says, that the eye cannot take in all at once will fail to please because "the unity and sense of the whole is lost for the spectator" (31).

Of course one wants to name exceptions; *The Cantos* please— if that's what they do—in part *because* the unity and sense of the whole is lost. But since size is fundamental to form, we have to acknowledge the smallness of poems as one of their primary formal characteristics. Not every poem is small, of course, but enough of them to justify the expectation. If Pound is right that "great literature is simply language charged with meaning to the utmost possible degree" (28), we could say that a poem, whatever form or shape it takes, is "language charged with meaning to the utmost possible degree, in the shortest amount of space." We could say most poems are supernovas: they must contract before they can explode:

> I dwell in Possibility—
> A fairer House than Prose—
> More numerous of Windows—
> Superior—for Doors—
>
> Of Chambers as the Cedars—
> Impregnable of eye—
> And for an everlasting Roof
> The Gambrels of the Sky—

> Of Visitors—the fairest—
> For Occupation—This—
> The spreading wide my narrow Hands
> To gather Paradise— (Dickinson 327)

Despite the domestic metaphor, this poem seems more black hole than house, those narrow hands part welcoming host, part event horizon, swallowing not just the cosmos but anyone hapless enough to get within a yard of the page.

We put texts in generic and formal boxes not because we love to tidy up, but because we love to notice leakages. Distinguishing between shapes is, therefore, a prerequisite to finding them beautiful. It is precisely because the membranes between the sonnet, the pastoral, the ballad, the bildungsroman, or the revenge tragedy are permeable that solidifying them matters. Similarly, the power of the small exists only in contrast with the big; it comes because we notice that a poem has been distilled out of the blob of background and accrued a diamond-hard circumference of its own.

Aristotle also argued that the problem of perspective worked the other way as well, that poems or animals that are too small aren't beautiful because we cannot see how their component parts comprise a unity. The haiku or the epigram might represent a certain limit, but I think poetry gets smaller still. Hollander's poem is proof that single words have music, and Linnaeus, who gave Latin names to more than thirteen thousand plants and animals, was in this regard a poet. (Hard to say what kind of strange homage was meant by using Aristotle's word, catharsis, for the turkey vulture: cathartes aura, "purifying wind.") Longinus claims even a phrase—"Let there be light"—can be sublime, can say it all, that even Ajax's silence can speak volumes and make Blake's grain of sand seem overdone.

6

In *Specimen Days* Whitman describes his 1879 trip to Colorado, and declares the impact of the Rocky Mountains on his art:

"I have found the law of my own poems," was the unspoken but more-and-more decided feeling that came to me as I pass'd, hour after hour...the chasm, the gorge, the crystal mountain stream, repeated scores, hundreds of miles—the broad handling and absolute uncrampedness—the fantastic forms, bathed in transparent browns, faint reds and grays, towering sometimes a thousand, sometimes two or three thousand feet high—at their tops now and then huge masses pois'd, and mixing with the clouds, with only their outlines, hazed in misty lilac, visible. (221)

Thoreau, in contrast, recalls his 1846 ascent up Maine's Mount Katahdin:

Perhaps I most fully realized that this was primeval, untamed, and forever untameable Nature...This was that Earth of which we have heard, made out of Chaos and Old Night. Here was no man's garden, but the unhandselled globe. It was not lawn, nor pasture, nor mead, nor woodland, nor lea, nor arable, nor waste-land. It was the fresh and natural surface of the planet Earth...It was Matter, vast, terrific...I stand in awe of my body, this matter to which I am bound has become so strange to me... rocks, trees, wind on our cheeks! The *solid* earth! the *actual* world! the *common sense*! *Contact! Contact! Who* are we? *where* are we? (33-34).

Whitman's epiphany is the solidification of the self and the aesthetic: "fantastic forms" remarkable in their "uncrampedness," a world in which an object's outlines never fully fade. In the passage by Thoreau, what gets solidified is erasure, not just of lawns, pastures, meads, or woodland, but Thoreau's own body, dissolved into a generalized and dislocated "we."

Thus the same kind of experience can produce two opposite outcomes. A mountain might command this kind of power over us more easily than anything, might make us feel that our stance on Earth is simultaneously both snug and slippery. But anything with a circumference can do it. I feel dizzy every time I read the sonnet by Edna St. Vincent Millay that begins: "I will put Chaos into fourteen lines / And keep him there" (153), because she gives to chaos concrete rhythm and deliberate heft. Because I realize that where there once was not-poem, there is now a poem. The language is more ordered than the language that surrounds it, than the air that surrounds it, though by all the laws of entropy it shouldn't be. A poem, any poem, presents us with a palpable shape, some foot-hold that has grown more stable by reminding me of how unstable I am. The poem is on the page, a whole made of component parts, distinct and solid in itself, and yet it reaches out to us to give it voice and vector: "I stop some where waiting for you" is its implicit final line, its outer edge.

Its ridges and clefts, its contours more than its content, are what determine how the wind sounds when it blows through them. Through us. They can make your flesh feel solid, and like it will melt.

The young avant-gardist should not think Blake's battle cry—"I must create a system or be enslaved by another man's"—is a get-out-of-form-free card. Blake's stance seems slightly less revolutionary when we notice that his poems are full of not just meter and rhyme, but sentences, and lines, and enjambments, and phrases, and grammar, and syntax, and punctuation, and rhythm, and words, and syllables, and ink. His poems are weird, but their component parts look just like everybody else's. Likewise the strict formalist has no real ammunition in Frost's quip about free verse being like playing tennis without a net. That only means that now you're playing something like racquetball, a game governed by just as many rules, not to mention the laws of physics. And if you haven't spent enough time polishing your backhand, you'll still lose. You can rebel against forms, in other words, but never form. Poems don't have forms. They *are* forms. Like that lady said about the turtles, it's form all the way down.

And we should be glad it is. Ovid's *omnia mutantur, nihil interit* is comforting until we realize it's just as true backwards as it is forwards: nothing dies, but everything changes. Too often chaos seems not only palpable, but total, and the sea of nothingness starts lapping, some days, at the top lip of the levee. Those November afternoons, for instance, when you doze off in some book and wake up drowning in an early dark, and for a panicked instant can't remember where you are, or when you are. You don't know where the darkness ends and you begin. You hear a siren, but you aren't sure if it's moving farther from you or if it's coming your way.

Bibliography

Aristotle. *Aristotle's Theory of Poetry and Fine Art: With a Critical Text and Translation of the Poetics.* Courier Corporation, 1951.

Dickinson, Emily. *The Complete Poems of Emily Dickinson.* Little Brown and Company, 1960.

Eliot, T. S. *Selected Essays.* Houghton Mifflin Harcourt, 2014.

Frye, Northrope. *Fables of Identity.* Harcourt, Brace & World, 1963.

Hass, Robert. *Twentieth Century Pleasures.* Ecco, 1984.

Hollander, John. *Selected Poems.* Secker and Warburg, 1972.

Hughes, Ted. *Tales from Ovid.* FSG, 1997.

Johnson, Samuel. *The Major Works.* Oxford University Press, 1984.

Kahn, Louis. *Essential Texts.* Norton, 2003.

Millay, Edna St. Vincent. *Collected Sonnets.* Harper Perennial, 1988.

Milton, John. *Paradise Lost.* Norton, 2005.

Pater, Walter. *The Renaissance: Studies in Art and Poetry.* University of California Press, 1980.

Pound, Ezra. *ABC of Reading.* New Directions Publishing, 1960.

Reeve, F. D. *Robert Frost in Russia*. Zephyr Press, 2001.

Rilke, Rainer Maria. *Duino Elegies*. FSG, 2000.

   —. *The Poetry of Rilke*. Macmillan, 2009.

Shelley, Percy Bysshe. *Shelley's Poetry and Prose*. Norton, 2002.

Thoreau, Henry David. *Elevating Ourselves: Thoreau on Mountains*. Houghton Mifflin Harcourt, 1999.

Whitman, Walt. *Specimen Days in America*. W. Scott, 1887.

Wordsworth, William. *The Prelude*. Norton, 1979.

Assisi

Mariel Glass

Evening rituals.
The yard buried in snow. A child napping in the other room.
Flowers in moonlight—
Speech-acts scraped from the aurality
Of fever. The short day is the brightest: frost
And fire—
The aphasia of the sun
In a long-abandoned cathedral.

Chapter 1.
At four o'clock, the milk-truck came (fifty
Years too late).
I wrote you several emails
Yesterday
Asking you to leave your house
For mine. Was this untowards? This single-minded
Pursuit of a real life?
Neighbors over for dinner, the TV on.

Winter in March means double-
Exposure: crisscrossing voices, negative Omegas, devotion
As thin as churchwafer.
It is a kind of innocence: the body that buries you,
Clings to you
And will not let you go.

But you will not talk to me, distrusting
Small graces—
The hypnotic glimmer
Of forgiveness,
The endless equipoise of famine.
So meaning is propelled inward. Questioned,
Gutted and husked—startled
Into flight.

Three Mediations of Reading Heraclitus
Michael Skelton

1. The first is hermeneutical. How are his hundred odd
fragments to be interpreted at the basic level of sense? Often I
will pass over a fragment of indeterminable, cryptic meaning
and feel the need to copy it down in my notebook. Take this
one, for example: (B90) All things are an exchange for fire
and fire for all things, as goods for gold and gold for goods.
What is it about this statement (which, to the twenty-first
century reader trained to metabolize tweet-sized thoughts,
should be nothing) that resonates long after I read it? No
doubt some of the effect comes from having read it as part of
a series of other statements structured just like it. Probably
its initial hold on me has less to do with the singularity of
its meaning than with its relation of dependency to these
other, equally suggestive statements. Repeating it several
times aloud, I start to feel that it is the strife between the
sense of this statement and its form that gives it its particular
resonance. The chiasmic structure of the statement does
not read like an attempt to repackage a pseudo-profundity
that is really without meaning. Rather, the chiasmus is itself
the meaning; the shape the thought takes is to some extent
its content. The transaction being spoken of, among things
and fire, fire and things, is modeled in the very grammar of
the chiasmus. And the relation between the chiasmus of the
first clause and that of the second produces an analogy that
helps me to extrapolate a bit of sense from the fragment: The
cosmos is an everlasting transaction between becoming and
unbecoming; fire is the currency of this transaction.

2. The second is philosophical. Many of Heraclitus' fragments exploit both the abundant ambiguities of classical Greek grammar and the relative poverty—at the time of his writing—of classical Greek's conceptual lexicon. What Heraclitus appears to be trying to work out in his philosophical fragments, then, is not the kind of systematic cosmology or epistemological treatise that we would expect to find in a medieval or modern philosopher, but a proverbial form of thinking that initiates—without fully completing—the translation of grammatical-poetical figures into the logical medium of concepts. Fragment B48: The name of the bow is life, but its work is death. As the translator notes, this fragment exploits the identical spelling of the classical Greek words for bow and life (bios). In speech, the two words would have received different accents, bow stressing the second syllable (biós), life stressing the first syllable (bíos). In writing, however, there were no diacritical marks to distinguish the two meanings. The reader would thus have had to perceive the play on words in order to begin interpreting the riddle. Such riddles are the medium of Heraclitus' thinking: translations-in-progress of figures into concepts, or what the author in other places calls "right thinking."

(Note: Heraclitus is generally critical of those who do not think in riddles with him. He believes that ordinary people are capable of it but are too lazy or poorly educated or otherwise indisposed to do it. He likewise believes that the educated elites of his time are not made wise by their vast learning. Their facts do not approach the level of understanding carried in the form of the riddle. For Heraclitus, then, the riddle is neither the property of the undereducated nor the overeducated, but belongs to any thinker who grasps the affinity between poetic figures and logical concepts—an affinity that, following him, seems to be buried in the deep grammar of language. Fragment B116: It belongs to all people to know themselves and to think rightly.)

3. The third is philological. What we know of Heraclitus we do not know from him directly. The compiled fragments we have today are sourced from spliced quotations and paraphrasings from other authors' texts. History has transformed Heraclitus from the fiercely independent thinker he is reported to have been in life into a total dependent on the intellectual projects of others. To be sure, many of those who quoted him did so out of admiration or agreement with what he wrote. But others no doubt exploited his name to validate claims that would have been weaker without an appeal to his authority. There is thus no "true" Heraclitus except the philological Heraclitus. Part of the task of reading him, beyond the hermeneutical and philosophical considerations I've mentioned, is to consult the source texts from which his sayings are compiled.

Fragment B93: The god whose oracle is at Delphi neither speaks nor conceals but gives a sign. As a floating fragment decontextualized from its source text, I take this to be a provisional definition of the riddle-medium in which Heraclitus' fragments are written. His riddle "signifies" like the Delphi oracle's sayings, neither disclosing meaning transparently nor withholding meaning opaquely. Just as when Apollo sends his cryptic messages through his Pythian oracle, the human supplicant is supposed to interpret the statement as best she is able, so the reader of Heraclitus is expected to mull over the words on the page without arriving at a fully determinate or fully indeterminate reading. In short, I read fragment B93 as an invitation into the world of Heraclitus' thinking, a riddle that helps to unravel his other riddles.

The source text of fragment B93 is Plutarch's On the Pythian Oracles, a dialogue written more than five centuries after Heraclitus' death, in which a man named Theon explains to his friends why the oracles at Delphi have ceased to speak in riddle-like verses, favoring a more immediately intelligible prose. Here is how the fragment appears in Plutarch's dialogue:

> For nothing seems better to reproduce the type, no instrument more obediently to use its own nature, than the moon. Yet taking from the sun his bright and fiery rays, she does not transmit them so to us: mingled with herself they change colour and also take on a different power; the heat wholly disappeared, and the light fails from weakness before it reaches us. I think you know the saying found in Heraclitus, that 'the sovereign whose seat is at Delphi, speaks not, nor conceals, but signifies.' Take and add then to what is here so well said, the conception that the God of this place employs the Pythia for the hearing as the sun employs the moon for the seeing. He shows and reveals his own thoughts, but shows them mingled in their passage through a mortal body, and a soul which cannot remain at rest or present itself to the exciting power unexcited and inwardly composed, but which boils and surges and is involved in the stirrings and troublesome passions from within.

The quotation is introduced to make the point that the god Apollo, when delivering his messages to the supplicants at Delphi, has always used the Pythian oracle in accordance with her particular faculties. At the time of Heraclitus' writing, the Pythian oracle was typically a woman of aristocratic breeding and education who would have know something of poetic composition and meter and would thus have been better prepared to deliver divine messages in high verse. The oracles of Plutarch's time, however, were typically peasant women without education, and were thus better suited to deliver Apollo's prophecies in plainer, more prosaic speech. But there was an additional reason for switching from poetic to prosaic prophecy beyond the social origin and education of the oracles: the supplications of the pilgrims at Delphi had fundamentally changed. In earlier times, according to Theon, pilgrims came to Apollo's temple at Delphi with dangerous and even daring inquiries, ones whose answers sometimes needed hiding from one's political enemies. The poetical obscurity of the prophecy hid its meaning from unwelcome eavesdroppers and spoke to the specific concerns of the supplicants, who, after applying their whole minds to the interpretation, were able to work the meaning out. In the present "settled condition" of the world, however (which, according to the speaker in the dialogue, is one in which "war has been made to cease" and peace and tranquility prevail), people come to the oracle with altogether different concerns. They worry about marriages, commercial transactions, and other quotidian affairs, asking fewer questions that might endanger their well being in the state. As Theon explains to his friends:

> Then there was a change in human life, affecting men both in fortune and in genius. Expediency banished what was superfluous, top-knots of gold were dropped, rich robes discarded; probably too clustering curls were shorn off, and the buskin

discontinued. It was not a bad training, to set the beauty of frugality against that of profusion, to account what was plain and simple, a better ornament than the pompous and elaborate. So it was with language: it changed with the times, and shared the general break-up. History got down from its coach, and dropped metre. Truth was best sifted out from Myth in prose; Philosophy welcomed clearness, and found it better to instruct than to astonish, so she pursued her inquiry in plain language. The God made the Pythia leave off calling her own fellow townsmen 'fire-burners', the Spartans 'serpent-eaters', men 'mountaineers', rivers 'mountain-drainers'. He cleared the oracle of epic verses, unusual words, circumlocutions, and vagueness, and so prepared the way to converse with his consultants just as law converses with states, as kings address subjects, as disciples hear their masters speak, so framing language as to be intelligible and convincing.

This shift from poetry to prose in oracular sayings appears to be a distinctively political achievement. The riddle-likeness of the earlier sayings of the oracle has been rendered unnecessary by a sea change in human beings' political relations to each other. Less imperiled in their public lives, they seek more banal guidance for their personal lives. Plutarch's citation of Heraclitus, assuming it is authentic, is likely a departure from the fragment's original meaning, and yet it provides the only context in which we can interpret that meaning. Once placed in a series with other Heraclitean fragments, it takes on another valence altogether.

(Final thought: the three mediations that must be attended to in Heraclitus's writings—the hermeneutical, the philosophical, the philological—are just magnifications of the demands that every text makes upon its reader.)

NOTE ON SOURCES

Citations of Heraclitus were taken from Cohen, Curd, & Reeve. Readings in Ancient Greek Philosophy: Fourth Edition. Hackett Publishing, Indianapolis: 2011. Citations of Plutatch were taken from http://penelope.uchicago.edu/misctracts/plutarchverses.html.

Archaic Democracy
Kelly M.S. Swope

For the past few years I have been trying to work out, in my thoughts and notebooks, a conclusive critical appraisal of the significance of democratic idealism in American writing. I admit that I have come to feel internally divided by the effort: one part of me seeks to continue drawing nourishment from writers who have been the most formative in my education, while another part of me seeks to put to rest a tradition that no longer responds to (even if it directly addresses) the political and cultural moment we inhabit. But before I go on, I should define my terms:

By democratic idealism I refer to a defunct tradition of political and cultural thinking that regarded American democracy as an essentially *imaginative* struggle unfolding alongside the *political* project of building egalitarian institutions by electoral consent. Among the deepest worries of the democratic idealist writers was the right of equally empowered minds to make consequential representations and judgments in the name of the entire *demos*. How could the individual literary genius work out the much-needed aesthetic synthesis of the sprawling, pluralistic mass? Who would be the common reader that could hold the literary genius accountable for her synthesis of the American manifold?

A beautiful symmetry binds this tradition, and its recurring questions, together. Idealism begins in the first half of the nineteenth century with Ralph Waldo Emerson's address to the young graduates of Harvard, "The American Scholar," and concludes, self-referentially, with Ralph Waldo Ellison's "The Little Man at Chehaw Station," an essay that appeared in 1978 in a magazine named for Emerson's Harvard address. Ellison's astonishing intimation of the symmetry between himself and his namesake, between the national culture of the twentieth century and the legacy of the nineteenth, and finally, between the Little Man and the American Scholar (two sides–audience and artist–of the same democratic coin), was, wittingly or not, an intimation that the idealist literary tradition, as well as the historical conditions that engendered it, were dying out with him.

Ellison was the last of the great idealists, and in the time since his most important writings, a host of non-idealist critical tendencies have taken the place of his stubborn faith in American democracy. This is not to say that certain vestiges of democratic idealism did not remain with a younger generation of writers who chose to carry Ellison's snuffed-out torch into a new age of democratic skepticism. Robert Pinsky, who was Poet Laureate of the United States (the highest honor for a so-called "civic poet") in the 1990s, is one such figure whose work arrests something important in the democratic idealist vision right at the moment of its vanishing. Pinsky's *An Explanation of America*, a book-length poem published the year after Ellison's "Little Man," shows a familiar propensity to represent American democracy as a sublime literary object while also cataloging the symptoms of a national culture aging out of its aspiration to give ever-new accounts of itself.

The recent memory of Vietnam casts a shadow over Pinsky's entire work; for the author, the war that nakedly exhibited America's ulterior interests in global affairs remolded the ambitious, inward-looking republic into the ages-old template of an empire become corrupt. "I think [Vietnam] made our country older, forever," he writes in a section of the poem called "Serpent Knowledge." "I don't mean better or not better, but merely/As though a person should come to a certain place/And have his hair turn gray, that very night." And a few lines later: "I think/That I may always feel as if I lived/In a time when the country aged itself:/More lonely together in our common strangeness…/As if we were a family, and some members/Had done an awful thing on a road at night…"

Pinsky's representation of the United States as aged and corrupted occurs alongside allusions to famous Roman battles and venerable Roman statesmen. A long section in *An Explanation of America*, for example, is written as if it were a letter from Horace to a friend concerning the duties of a citizen to his republic. References to ancient Greek literature crop up throughout the poem as well. In one section, "Bad Dreams," Homer's Odysseus comes to replace Walt Whitman as the ur-figure of the American poet taking account of the national landscape:

> That quiet leads me to a stranger's dread/Of the place frightened settlers might invent:/The customs of the people there, the tongues/They speak, and what they have to drink, the things/That they imagine, might falter in such a place,/Or be too few; and men would live like Cyclopes,/"With neither assemblies nor any settled customs"-/Or Laestrygonians who consume their kind/And see a stranger as his meat and marrow,/And have no cities or cultivated farms.

Pinsky's frequent substitution of classical tropes for "American" ones extinguishes the sense of the United States as a country forever coming of age. In his poetry, democracy loses its open-ended, unhistorical freedom and becomes a historical prison for the incompletely emancipated. He writes of America's "mellowing to another country/Of different people living in different places," as if to suggest that, finally, enough past has accumulated behind the United States that it can now give a sober account of itself. "The accumulating prison of the past/ Pulls us toward a body and a place," he writes, "a plural headed Empire, manifold/Beyond my outrage or admiration." The sobering accumulations of the past work together with the numerous classical allusions in the poem. Reading Pinsky, one gets the impression that ahead of the United States lie more inimitable achievements, both political and cultural, but also, like the great civilizations of the ancient world, more senseless wars, the inevitable entropy of empire, and a universalized "suffering that could [not] make us wiser,/or nobler, but only older, and more ourselves..."

The backward-looking classicism of *An Explanation of America* finds its corollary in the archaic psychologism of an important later essay by Pinsky called *Democracy, Culture and the Voice of Poetry*. First given as a lecture in 2001, the essay defines the current crisis of democratic culture in terms of primitive-seeming anxieties that are actually symptoms of democracy's maturation: in one direction, democracy fears being unjustifiably dominated or coerced into a universal conformism that effaces difference; in the other direction, it fears over-differentiation, a diversification so diffuse that it cannot be gathered under a single proper name. "Historical memory," Pinksy suggests, "tempers both of the[se] imagined extremes of culture":

Memory resists uniformity because it registers fine gradations; memory resists the factional because it registers the impure, recombining, fluent nature of culture. It is memory that eventually undermines the apparently total successes of both the colonizing Conquistador and the leveling Visigoth. The fantastic element in democratic memory exaggerates the anxieties of uniformity and fragmentation. Accustomed to practicing an ancient, singular art amid a dazzling mass culture, the American poet is a kind of veteran of these anxieties.

Archaic anxieties and the ancient art of poetry find a common home in Pinsky's backward-looking, memorialist outlook. For him, poetry discloses the evolving historical tensions between universalism and particularism, individual and mass, within the "mellowing" American psyche. The poet's *vocal* medium is her chief asset in fulfilling this social task. "In a poem," writes Pinksy, "the social realm is invoked with a special intimacy at the barely voluntary level of voice itself. Communal life, whether explicitly included or not, is present implicitly in the cadences and syntax of language: a somatic ghost." This duality of solitary voice and ghostlike community—a duality that Pinsky repeatedly analogizes to the experience of democracy itself—has been with humanity since the first intentional sounds rolled off the human tongue. For, just like every poet before her, today's American poet is nothing more than a solitary voice trying to overhear herself—trying, out of freedom and loneliness, to simulate a third-person's empathy for her solitude—with rare affirmations of success.

It seems that, for Pinsky, poetry alone teaches the aging democratic citizen that the historical apotheosis of self-representation is in fact a reversion to an archaic struggle between voice and community, solitude and communal belonging. In its national poetry, American democracy magnifies tensions inherited from the most ancient human civilizations and creates a repository of mythical memory that attends far less to the empirical events of history than to the structuring dualities of the imagination. In the conceptual refinement of Pinksy's arguments, one can sense his break with the more impressionistically minded democratic idealists that came before him. Having inherited their questions as something historically other than his own, he can now speak with a measured retrospection, as someone older, more jaded, than they. It is in this way that his reflections on the classical, even archaic, strains within American life expose the basically adolescent conception of democracy that belonged to the idealists. His poetry summarizes better than the critic can why his predecessors began to disappear with the first confirmations of their country's irreversible aging.

NOTE ON SOURCES

Poetry citations are from Robert Pinksy, *An Explanation of America*, Princeton University Press, 1979. Essay citations are from Robert Pinsky, *Democracy, Culture and the Voice of Poetry*, Princeton University Press, 2002.

Notes on Book 1 of the Odyssey; or, Telemakhos' Bedroom

Joseph Magnus

At the beginning of the Odyssey, Odysseus is trapped on a beautiful, wooded island at the

navel of the sea by the beautiful, deadly goddess Kalypso, in her hollow, vaulted cave;

at the end of Book 1, Telemakhos is wrapped in a fine ram's fleece on his bed in his beautiful,

densely made bedroom, mulling over in his mind the charge from the goddess Athena to go

find out about his father;

the word describing Telemakhos' wrapped-ness is 'kekalummenos', which shares the Proto-

Indo-European root *kel- with 'Kalypso';

the Greek verb that uses this root is 'kalupto': to hide, conceal, cover, veil, and (tellingly) bury,

as at death;

*kel- became 'hell' in English, by the way.

Telemakhos' bedroom is described as 'puka poietos';

'puka' (adverbial here) is dense, compact, closely arranged, like perfectly made joints in a piece of wooden furniture, and (more metaphorically) it points to wisdom and shrewdness and

wiliness and care;

'poietos' means 'made'; 'poiesis', 'fabrication, creation, production';

English borrowed 'poetry' from here.

'Puka poietos' is used another time about three quarters of the way through the book to

describe the ceiling of the main hall of Odysseus' home;

at that point, Penelopeia, Odysseus' human wife, stands by the weight-bearing pillar that holds

up this well-made roof as she begs the bard to stop singing about the homecoming hardships

of the Akhaian heroes;

her husband hasn't returned, and her heart can't take the reminder;

speaking of pillars, Kalypso's daddy is that famous character Atlas who scans and sees the

depths of all the seas and holds the pillars that hold the earth and the sky;

I should mention the word for 'hold' is 'ekho', as in 'to have and to hold (marriage?), keep, be in

charge of, maintain, support'...

When Athena comes to Ithaka from her Olympian home, the spear she carries is mentioned 4 times in 30 lines (3 full lines are dedicated to describing it);

at last Telemakhos takes it from her and leans it against a pillar in the spear case which holds

Odysseus' many spears which are all standing at attention, waiting for his return obviously.

~~~~

the sky with its celestial bodies of day and night, which give the ones who die their sense of

time and location, which make the sea navigable, the 'puka poietos' sky;

'puka poietos'=densely packed? meaningfully packed?

the narrow, focused power of a spear, a pillar, a soldier at attention / the encompassing,

comforting, divining flatness of the sky, a ceiling, a bedroom;

I haven't even mentioned doors and thresholds…or song and dance…the falling of night…or

hosting and guesting…

our space is our mind is our world is our life is our self is our

poetry

'poiesis'

Puka poietos.

Puka poietos.

-ARCHY: a manifesto
Sam Corbin

Cast of Characters:

At home:

PATRIARCH
MISS AGRETHA SIEVE, his wife
THESAURUS & ANTONYM, their conjoined twin sons
READYMAID, the housekeeper
EULOGIST, a door-to-door eulogist

Around the hospital:

DOCTOR
NURSE
WOMAN, played by the actor
    who plays MISS AGRETHA SIEVE
NOTAMAN, an Ottoman

In the forest:

BEFORETUNE, a before-tune teller
RUSSELL, a foley artist
SUBJUNCTIVE (aka Jeff), the irrealis mood
GRAPEVINE, a quick-step
ARCHIVIST
MUSCLE, played by the actor who plays RUSSELL

At Wit's End:

KING FORM
REASON, played by the actor
    who plays MISS AGRETHA SIEVE
MNEMONIST, played by the actor
    who plays PATRIARCH
THE DEVIL
DISBELIEF, a prisoner

MISS SIEVE

Then again, able to! No, that isn't wouldn't have been able
won't have been? No, once you had, you wouldn't be right.
Once you have, you to. No…once you are, you…

PATRIARCH

Aggy.

*With some effort MISS SIEVE produces a strange-
looking contraption from under her skirts, almost like
a viewfinder.*

MISS SIEVE

They delivered it today.

PATRIARCH

What is that?

MISS SIEVE

I found it.

PATRIARCH

Did not.

MISS SIEVE

Did so. In the guesthouse.

PATRIARCH

What were you doing in the guesthouse?

MISS SIEVE

Musing.

PATRIARCH

How very unlike you.

MISS SIEVE

Yes, somewhat beneath me.

On the way to the door, READYMAID encounters
THESAURUS & ANTONYM, who tumble into her
path as they fight. Ad libs of "Did not! Did too!" She
jumps as they almost bowl her over.

READYMAID

Boys! What are you fighting about?

THESAURUS

Readymaid! Readymaid! Tony cheated!

ANTONYM

Did not!

THESAURUS

Did so!

ANTONYM

Did not!

THESAURUS

Did so!

ANTONYM

Did not!

THESAURUS

Did not!

ANTONYM

Did so!

THESAURUS

Did not!

ANTONYM

Did so!

THESAURUS

Did not!

READYMAID

Boys, you know your father gets nervous when you can't be accounted for.

THESAURUS

Why can't you account us?

ANTONYM

Anybody can do that. *(Pointing to himself, then his brother)* One, two.

THESAURUS

That's not what she meant!

ANTONYM

Is so!

THESAURUS

Is not!

ANTONYM

Is so!

THESAURUS

Is not!

ANTONYM

Is so!

THESAURUS

Is so!

ANTONYM

Is not!

READYMAID

Boys, go and sit in the parlor with your father. We have a guest.

ANTONYM

Guest who?

THESAURUS

A wild guest! I love a wild guest!

*They run off into the parlor. READYMAID goes to the
door. From the other side, unseen:*

EULOGIST

Knock knock.

READYMAID

Who's there?

EULOGIST

Opportunity.

READYMAID

Opportunity who?

EULOGIST

It's the eulogist.

READYMAID

Eulogist who?

EULOGIST

If eulogist open the door—

READYMAID

I don't know a eulogist.

EULOGIST

Allow me to introduce myself, then.

READYMAID

You already did. You're the eulogist.

EULOGIST

And whom do I have the pleasure?

READYMAID

I'm the housekeeper.

EULOGIST

Already something we have in common.

READYMAID

You keep house?

EULOGIST

I'm in the service industry.

READYMAID

What kind of service do you provide?

EULOGIST

It's more of a sermon.

(beat)

READYMAID

Who did you say you were?

The PATRIARCH appears behind her and thrusts open the door, revealing the EULOGIST, who looks somewhat surprised to see the PATRIARCH standing there. He recovers.

PATRIARCH

Why, it's the Eulogist!

READYMAID

Why is it the eulogist?

PATRIARCH

I'm glad it's not just anyone.

EULOGIST

What's the matter, Pat? You got a problem with ambiguity?

THE PATRIARCH ushers READYMAID ahead with the EULOGIST behind; he remains in the rear. READYMAID tries to look behind her as they file into the parlor where MISS SIEVE sits, now hiding something under her skirts.

PATRIARCH

Boys! Ag! The Eulogist is here!

MISS SIEVE

The eulogist! How nice. I could use a good eulogy; I've been feeling so terribly sensitive.

EULOGIST

I'm here on different orders today, ma'am. No words, only pictures. Then again, you know what they say!

MISS SIEVE

That's why I wanted to hear what you say!

EULOGIST

I'm afraid I can't be of service today.

MISS SIEVE

Not even a short service? Not a verse?

EULOGIST

Not averse, just assigned. On call.

MISS SIEVE

I don't want the on-call-ogist, I want—

PATRIARCH

Aggy.

EULOGIST

I'm here to deliver a parcel. It's an appliance for Archy-funded salaried households.

He pulls out the machine. MISS SIEVE and the
PATRIARCH exchange a glance.

EULOGIST

Nifty little thing. They're calling it the Retrospect!

PATRIARCH

What does it do?

EULOGIST

It generates alternative outcomes to events that have
already taken place. You can adjust the focus so it gets more
and more trivial, or more and more banal. For example, you
could generate something as minute as alternatives to, say,
the word alternative.

EULOGIST passes the viewfinder to the twins, who
have been grabby-handing this whole time. They look
inside.

THESAURUS

Stunt doubles!

ANTONYM

Stand-ins!

THESAURUS

Understudies!

ANTONYM

Replacements!

THESAURUS

Substitutes!

ANTONYM

Second opinions!

They giggle, passing it back to the EULOGIST.

EULOGIST

And on this side you can turn this knob to widen the scope of the road not taken, the road-o-scope. Calibrated, of course, to suit varying degrees of nostalgia.

MISS SIEVE

Is it safe?

EULOGIST

Very safe appliance, never short-circuits. And if you don't like what you see, *(he looks at READYMAID),* simply pull the reliever lever.

PATRIARCH

(going towards one of the levers on the toy) This reliever lever?

EULOGIST

NO! No, that's the re-liver lever. Don't want to touch that one.

MISS SIEVE

Why not?

EULOGIST

(lying) Factory settings. Don't want to reset the thing by accident. You'd have to recalibrate and recalculate and recapitulate and if there's anything you should do only once in your life, it's capitulate!

MISS SIEVE

Now that's the eulogist I love and remember!

EULOGIST

In any case, I've got to go door to door. Big shipment. No charge, of course. But do be careful with it. Not a toy, boys.

THESAURUS & ANTONYM

Aw!

EULOGIST

You take good care of that thing. Every family gets one.

EULOGIST goes to leave, then stops and looks at READYMAID.

EULOGIST

Every family gets one.

He exits. A silence. Then:

MISS SIEVE

Why did we get two, then?

PATRIARCH

Aggy!

MISS SIEVE

What?

READYMAID

Why would we have two?

MISS SIEVE

We don't.

PATRIARCH

Because you got one, Readymaid.

READYMAID

Me?

MISS SIEVE

From the guesthouse.

READYMAID

I have a Retrospect? Where is it?

MISS SIEVE

Nevermind where it is. It's nowhere.

PATRIARCH

Agretha Sieve. Do not use that word in this house.

READYMAID

I'd like to see it.

PATRIARCH

Aggy, if we have two—

MISS SIEVE

We don't have to do anything. You saw how it works, Pat. She'd only be wallowing in self-pity after she saw the alternative.

READYMAID

/How do you know that?

MISS SIEVE

What?

READYMAID

How do you know what life I might have led? Did you see something in my Retrospect?

PATRIARCH

Aggy, give the thing here, I'd like to see.

READYMAID

With all due respect—

MISS SIEVE

Don't be rude.

MISS SIEVE goes over to PATRIARCH and attempts to extract READYMAID's Retrospect from under her skirts.

READYMAID

I've a right to my self-pity.

MISS SIEVE

(ignoring her) Pat, let's reset the thing.

Removing the RETROSPECT proves to be extremely difficult, and MISS SIEVE suddenly behaves as if she is going into labor. Sounds crescendo.

MISS SIEVE

AGH! AGHH!

PATRIARCH

Aggy!

READYMAID

I feel…

THESAURUS

What's mommy doing?

ANTONYM

She's dying!

THESARUS.

Is not!

ANTONYM

Is so!

THESAURUS

Is not!

Lights flicker as MISS SIEVE pushes. The sound is deafening. Lights explode. A sonic tear, and a blackout. MISS SIEVE's cries continue and slowly blend into another WOMAN's cries.

Scene II

A hospital delivery room. The scene is tight and spotlit, so that the stage around it is in blackness. A WOMAN on the delivery table, in labor. A DOCTOR and NURSE stand poised, attempting to deliver. The woman on the table screams in pain.

DOCTOR

Push!

WOMAN

AGHH!

NURSE

Nothing.

WOMAN

YOU CALL THIS NOTHING?

NURSE

I don't see a head...

WOMAN

Is that all? GOD, BLESS THIS NURSE WITH FORESIGHT.

NURSE

(walking away) I can't work like this.

WOMAN

Oh look, she's on MATERNITY LEAVE.

DOCTOR

I need calm, you two. I can't work under these conditions.

WOMAN

What about over them?

DOCTOR

Listen Mrs...

WOMAN

…Can't…remember.

DOCTOR

Mrs. Can't Remember. We won't be able to proceed/

WOMAN

WHAT/

DOCTOR

/with a conventional birth. You're too narrow.

WOMAN

Dilate me, then! Give me a wide birth!

DOCTOR

That won't do either. It seems as though the baby inside of you is already fully formed.

(beat)

WOMAN

I should hope so!

DOCTOR

I mean that it has the features of a grown woman.

WOMAN

[…]

DOCTOR

Sorry, I'm not being clear. It is a grown woman.

WOMAN screams and passes out, possibly dead. After a silence:

NURSE

A little dramatic.

DOCTOR

(checking her pulse) She's not breathing. We'll have to perform a C-section.

NURSE

But I still don't see anything.

DOCTOR

Nurse, we've got a womb full of people waiting for us to deliver and by God, I'm going to deliver!

NURSE

People? There's more than one?

DOCTOR

There are two.

NURSE

Are not.

DOCTOR

Are two.

NURSE

Are not.

DOCTOR

What's gotten into you?

NURSE

I'm sorry, I don't know. I think, *(has forgotten his own name)*, I'm having…déja-vu? *(beat)* Why didn't you tell her about the second?

DOCTOR

She didn't seem like she could bear it.

NURSE

She's already bearing it.

WOMAN moans, coming to.

WOMAN

Can't… won't…would've…could've..

DOCTOR

It's the contractions, they're quickening. We've got to act fast. Scalpel!

NURSE hands a scalpel. DOCTOR works. WOMAN moans.

DOCTOR

Forceps!

NURSE hands the forceps. DOCTOR works. WOMAN moans.

DOCTOR

Sutures!

NURSE hands the sutures. DOCTOR works. WOMAN moans.

DOCTOR

You know it's very easy to self-suture.

NURSE

Suit yourself.

DOCTOR

To each his own.

NURSE

'Til each is sown.

DOCTOR reaches into the woman's belly. A sound begins that grows in intensity. WOMAN screams as DOCTOR extracts two babies. One is a baby-looking baby, which he hands to the NURSE. One is a fully grown woman: It is READYMAID. She emerges from underneath the delivery blanket, wet but fully clothed and unbloodied. WOMAN on the table dies. A low buzzing sound begins.

DOCTOR

Delivery!

The NURSE is holding the baby but breathless at the sight of something we cannot see, as though there is an unseen figure standing near where READYMAID is standing.

NURSE

(in awe) Deliverance!

The buzzing continues to grow in intensity. READYMAID looks around, bewildered at the scene.

DOCTOR

(checking the woman's pulse) Dear God.

READYMAID

Excuse me.

NURSE

Doctor, I feel strange.

DOCTOR

Nurse, this woman isn't feeling at all.

NURSE

Harsh.

DOCTOR

Sorry, I'm not being clear. She's dead.

READYMAID

Excuse me, did I just come out of...?

They do not hear her. The Doctor/Nurse scene continues in silent ad-libs as if she isn't there. Buzzing grows in intensity.

READYMAID walks across the stage and the buzzing recedes. The lights come up on a very sparsely furnished room stage right, nondescript and nowhere in particular. No furniture in the room save for a spinny chair, a telephone and an ottoman—NOTAMAN—with an sign that says "NOTAMAN". The spinny chair turns to reveal the EULOGIST, wearing a name tag that says "EULOGIST". It is partially covered under a rumpled suit jacket.

READYMAID

You!

EULOGIST gestures to the other syllables of his name.

EULOGIST

Lo-gist.

READYMAID

I don't see the "-gist."

EULOGIST

That's why I'm here to give it to you, Readymaid.

READYMAID

You know my name?

EULOGIST

Call it a wild guess.

READYMAID

I don't think I ought to. Am I dead?

EULOGIST

Doubtful. And I'd be the first to know. Come, let's chat. Come and have a seat on the NOTAMAN.

READYMAID goes and sits down. Audible or visible grunt of discomfort from the NOTAMAN.

READYMAID

(*dusting herself off*) I imagine you're going to tell me what I just saw.

EULOGIST

You tell me. I didn't see anything.

READYMAID

Just now, when I came out of a person?

EULOGIST

A last wheeze from the Retrospect. Shows you a moment from your life you can't change right before the moment you can.

READYMAID

So I've been reborn? (*beat*) Was that my mother, then?

EULOGIST nods.

EULOGIST

Resilient as anything.

READYMAID

My birth broke character, I take it.

EULOGIST

When she died, do you know who was made privy to her eulogy?

READYMAID

The Sieves?

EULOGIST

Her service and yours, to the highest-bidding family in town. You're very special, Readymaid. Do you know that?

READYMAID

Well, that was quite the scene of revelation. And I do feel somewhat as though I've had a renaissance.

NOTAMAN coughs involuntarily. EULOGIST kicks
it. NOTAMAN wheezes. READYMAID looks down.

NOTAMAN

I mean…*(attempting to cover up by making the sound a piece of furniture makes)* cooouch?

Everyone dismisses this, scene continues.

EULOGIST

And you never wondered why they took to you so quickly, The Sieves?

READYMAID

I wasn't aware they took to me. I've been at their estate for as long as I can remember. Though it's always felt like a very transitive position.

EULOGIST

When in reality, it was transitory.

READYMAID

I guess you looked inside my Retrospect, too.

EULOGIST

What do you mean, too?

READYMAID

Seems as if everyone but me has had the chance.

EULOGIST

That can't be right.

READYMAID

I do feel very left out.

EULOGIST

You mean you didn't pull the re-liver lever?

READYMAID

Now you're telling me I'm supposed to fulfill some kind of destiny as a free woman.

EULOGIST

Who did, then?

READYMAID

I don't understand. I've been made to start again without any indications of where to go next. How am I to know what I was meant to do?

NOTAMAN

(from underneath her) I'll tell you!

>*READYMAID gasps and suddenly stands up, NOTAMAN shifts and stands up, throwing off his cover.*

EULOGIST

Notaman!

READYMAID

(in utter shock) The not-a-man's a lotta-man! The chair's got hair! The settee's a HE!

NOTAMAN

That's right!

>*He flips his sign around to reveal the word "AREAMAN."*

EULOGIST

(reading) Area man?

NOTAMAN

No, ARE -a-man! As in, you ARE a man...*(he rips the whole thing off in frustration)* You know what, it doesn't matter. I'm putting in my notice.

NOTAMAN pulls out a sign that says "NOTICE" and extends it to the EULOGIST.

NOTAMAN

And I expect you to take it.

EULOGIST

(snubbing his nose) I certainly won't take notice.

NOTAMAN

Sir, with all due respect, I may be your footstool but I'm no doormat.

EULOGIST

Notaman, no. Think of the coffee stains. The time I tickled you until I found enough loose change to do my laundry.

NOTAMAN

Sir, I've been a humble appurtenance in this parlor for as long as I can remember. But I've spent far too long on all fours and it's time to take a stand, and give these arms rest.

EULOGIST

I can't believe I'm hearing this.

NOTAMAN

I used to think all I wanted was a table's income, a comfortable lifestyle. But I've since bolstered my confidence, and I'm ready to throw cushion to the wind. I've been inspired by Readymaid's tale of rebirth. And I wish to join her on her quest.

READYMAID

Quest? What quest?

NOTAMAN

The one in question. The quest to overcome.

READYMAID

Overcome what?

EULOGIST

Heard enough. Won't have it. Can't part with the furniture.

READYMAID

I wasn't aware of a quest.

NOTAMAN

I'm tired of being objectified! I will quest alongside Readymaid as a fellow work of art.

READYMAID

Work of art?

NOTAMAN

I may not be as rare as she, but I'm told I'm quite the hot commode.

EULOGIST

Commodity.

NOTAMAN

It's French.

READYMAID

(remembering her own name) I'm French.

NOTAMAN and EULOGIST stop and look at READYMAID.

(beat)

READYMAID

French made.

EULOGIST

(encouraging her) That's it, Readymaid.

READYMAID

Née du champ. Borne afield.

EULOGIST

Born in full, ready-made.

READYMAID

All this time, I had it "maid."

EULOGIST

You misheard. Happens to the best of us.

NOTAMAN

But only to the best of us.

READMAID.

E suis moi-même.

EULOGIST

And others will, too.

READYMAID

Now you've lost me.

NOTAMAN

You're a prophet, Readymaid.

READYMAID

(beat) Is there a prophecy?

EULOGIST turns to NOTAMAN.

EULOGIST

Notaman, if this is how you really feel, then go. Join Readymaid on her quest.

He takes the "NOTICE" sign from NOTAMAN.

READYMAID

What quest?

EULOGIST

Begs the question, doesn't it?

The phone rings. It sounds identical to all the bells we heard in Scene I.

EULOGIST

Sorry, I'm on-call.

The EULOGIST goes to the phone and picks it up. He listens into the receiver, then holds out the phone to READYMAID.

EULOGIST

It's for you.

READYMAID

For me?

READYMAID doesn't move.

READYMAID

I don't want it.

EULOGIST

It's your call.

READYMAID

I know, and no, thank you.

EULOGIST

It might tell you what you want to know.

READYMAID

I don't want to know any of this. I want to un-know. I want an annulment.

EULOGIST

Readymaid, you can't divorce yourself from your purpose now.

READYMAID

I was fine before I knew I had one.

EULOGIST

So, the art objects!

READYMAID

It does.

EULOGIST

Readymaid.

READYMAID

(correcting him) Readymade.

> *READYMAID takes the receiver from the EULOGIST and holds the phone to her ear. We can hear the curly, muffled sounds of a voice on the other side of the line but cannot make out what is said. Eventually, she hands the receiver back to the EULOGIST.*

NOTAMAN

Who was it?

READYMAID

(honestly) It was automated.

EULOGIST

What did they say?

> *READYMAID stares at EULOGIST.*

READYMAID

You know what they say.

EULOGIST

Do not.

READYMAID

Do too. This is your receiving line. What's the -Archy?

EULOGIST

(pause) I do wish I could tell you, Readymaid. *(pause, thinking.)* Well I could tell you, but I'd have to kill you. *(pause, thinking.)* First. I'd have to kill you first, and then tell everyone else what kind of person you were meant to be.

READYMAID

And what kind of person is that?

EULOGIST

A messiah.

READYMAID

THE messiah?

EULOGIST

Not one that's existed before.

READYMAID

What does that have to do with an -Archy?

EULOGIST

I can't talk about that.

READYMAID

Not even in part?

READYMAID

Why not?

EULOGIST

Because the -Archy is the ultimate metaphor, far greater than the sum of its parts. Its very existence is an obstruction.

READYMAID

And mine an abstraction.

EULOGIST

Yes. The -Archy's presence is as pervasive as yours, but it has its own Constitution. Constituents. Omnipotence. Obituaries. *(beat)* I shouldn't be talking about this.

The phone rings.

EULOGIST

You'd better go. I'm sorry I couldn't be of more service.

He picks up the phone.

NOTAMAN

(to READYMAID) I can be a surface!

NOTAMAN poses as an ottoman again.

READYMAID

That's alright, Notaman. Let's go.

NOTAMAN and READYMAID exit as the EULOGIST watches. Lights shift to follow them as the scene dissolves around them.

Scene III

NOTAMAN and READYMAID re-emerge, mindlessly entering a large forest. The lights have dimmed, so there is an ominous feeling to the woods. They pass a sign that reads "The Forest of Whimsy".

NOTAMAN

That was quite the scene of relevation.

READYMAID

You mean revelation?

They pass another that reads "Abandon all sense, ye who enter here".

NOTAMAN

Nope. I was on all fours, and now I'm upright. Finally relevated to a standing vocation.

READYMAID

I hadn't thought of that. What will you do now?

They pass a sign that reads something incomprehensible.

NOTAMAN

Not sure. I was so swept up in the rush of quitting the crush of sitting for so long in one place. *(beat)* I wonder if I'll be replaced.

A fortune teller-type—BEFORETUNE—has been following unobtrusively the entire time.

BEFORTUNE

That's very moving.

READYMAID jumps and NOTAMAN goes full table.

READYMAID

Where did you come from?

BEFORTUNE

I could certainly tell you, but that wouldn't be of any use to you.

READYMAID

I'd feel...Notaman!

NOTAMAN gets up and dusts himself off.

NOTAMAN

Sorry, reflex.

READYMAID

I'd feel a little less jarred knowing you didn't pop out of thin air.

BEFORTUNE

Maybe I did. What's the sense in knowing?

READYMAID

None, I suppose. My own peace of mind.

NOTAMAN

(still spooked) I'd give her a piece of my mind...

READYMAID

Who are you?

BEFORTUNE

I'm Beforetune, the great contextualizer. I give you a clearer picture of what you're up against by providing a little background.

NOTAMAN

Sounds redundant.

READYMAID

Notaman! *(turning his back)* Excuse him. He's still adjusting to life as a free divan.

BEFORTUNE

In order to discover the lay of the land, you'll need to know about its laws, fallible though they may be.

READYMAID

Go on, we're listening.

NOTAMAN

(still spooked) She's listening.

BEFORTUNE

Once upon a time—and I say "a Time" quite specifically, since before the -Archy there wasn't any agreement about Time as an Absolute, let alone something which moved in any one direction or another. But once—or perhaps probably more than once, probably an infinite number of moments laid alongside one another...

NOTAMAN

Would you mind getting to the point?

BEFORTUNE

There is no point.

READYMAID

What?

BEFORTUNE

There are a number of points. Or there were, anyway, until someone came along and deemed them a Line. But now I've skipped ahead, and that's categorically against the law.

READYMAID

Against the law!

BEFORTUNE

We'll begin at the beginning—it's safer there.

READYMAID

Safer?

BEFORTUNE

My dear, if you echo everything I'm saying we'll only get half as far.

READYMAID says nothing.

BEFORTUNE

There was a time, before the -Archy, when an object was accepted as only being seen from its own side. The world was a subjective undertaking, and consensus was entirely a matter of coincidence.

NOTAMAN

Like a chemical reaction!

BEFORTUNE

That's a coincidence of matter. This is different. Everyone was mostly carefree, taking care only not to misrepresent what they were seeing in the company of others. Everything a matter of representation, and everyone a free agent.

NOTAMAN

(to READYMAID) I said it was chemical.

BEFORTUNE

And because no one saw the world quite in the same version, no one was particularly interested in valuing one version over another, either.

READYMAID

So there was no one version.

BEFORTUNE.

A version wasn't an issue. Then—and I don't know quite what I mean by "then," but the Law of Narrative Continuity demands it—then one day, someone came forward and declared that objects could be deduced without being seen. He claimed every object was subject to the same principle. He called this principle "Form." Eventually, he called himself Form.

READYMAID

Just…Form? Not short for anything?

BEFORTUNE

No. And everyone liked this notion of short Form very much. And it was innocent enough, at first. Meetings were held, where people would describe objects they had seen and try to find common ground with one another. Common ground led to common sense, and words like etcetera were needed to an increasing degree.

NOTAMAN

Why?

BEFORTUNE

Because once something had been defined, or deduced, or explained away, the matter itself was deemed redundant.

READYMAID

Even if it bore repeating?

BEFORTUNE

Repetition itself became a bore, and was soon abhorred by everyone. Meanwhile, Form grew ever more stringent, appointing himself a rule so that he always applied.

READYMAID

What about exceptions?

BEFORTUNE

There were a few of those, but they only proved his rule. Wit and Whimsy were two of them. Whimsy was neglected and untended, and became the gangled forest you find yourselves in now. Wit lay just beyond; Form cut clear through it until he found *(whisper)* Wit's End. And he created a hermitage there, at the edge of a world nobody had ever conceived of having edges.

NOTAMAN

That doesn't make sense. Everything has edges.

BEFORTUNE

Eventually Form did away with sense entirely and appointed Reason in its place. Misunderstandings were no longer open to interpretation. Statements came to be known as categorically true or false, good or bad. And there was so much fuss with everyone trying to make snap judgments that the Devil came to town.

READYMAID

The Devil? As in the devil, you know?

BEFORTUNE

No, the devil you don't. It was much worse. This devil wasn't so much an extremist as a futilist, a tautology brought about by everyone else's circular attempts to justify. He took court at *(whisper)* Wit's End as the hopelessness of all hope.

NOTAMAN

That's intense.

BEFORTUNE

He was the cruelest intention. Laws like Narrative Continuity came into effect. Beginnings were heavily taxed and deemed prerequisites to finding any middle ground, so compromise fell out of use.

READYMAID

Not even to agree to disagree?

BEFORTUNE

No one could afford it. Form claimed his rule even applied to something as abstract as time itself. Time had edges, and he claimed he could see it from all its sides. Subjective experience was deemed punishable by death.

READYMAID

Death!

BEFORTUNE

After a number of executions and failed objections, everyone finally gave in. The gates to *(whisper)* Wit's End swung shut so no one but the -Archy could know the methods of their madness. And that, my dears, is the Myth of Objectivity. I think you're all caught up now.

NOTAMAN

(snapping out of it) Oh wow, I was. It was a very good story.

BEFORTUNE

I should hope so. I'm a teller, after all. *(noticing READYMAID)* You seem withdrawn, my dear.

READYMAID

(pause) Well, to be perfectly honest with you, Miss Fortune—

BEFORTUNE

Be-fortune.

READYMAID

I'm not sure what that all should mean to me.

BEFORTUNE

That's a question only a mood can answer.

READYMAID

A mood?

BEFORTUNE

In a manner of speaking.

READYMAID

Speaking of manners, you'll have to forgive mine.

She extends her hand.

READYMAID

I'm/ Readymaid.

BEFORTUNE

Readymade.

READYMAID

You know my name?

BEFORTUNE

Less important that I know it, and moreso that you do.

READYMAID

I know my own name.

BEFORTUNE

Remember it. You still have to be Ready for what's coming.

READYMAID

Which is?

BEFORTUNE

Oh, I can't see ahead. I'm just a Beforetune Teller, before-shadowing the future by offering a contrast in the past imperfect.

READYMAID

Well, so far you're the second person who's told me I'm destined to save everybody from this -Archy, and I'm certainly amenable to the idea. But I still don't feel as if I've found a greater purpose.

BEFORTUNE

Oh, is that all? Here, you can have one of mine.

BEFORETUNE takes a rock from her pocket and hands it to READYMAID.

NOTAMAN

Hey, that's just a rock!

BEFORTUNE

I know it's not quite what you're looking for, but you can use it for now until you find a better one.

READYMAID takes the rock.

READYMAID

Thank you.

BEFORTUNE

My jurisdiction ends presently, so I've got to go now! Good luck!

She somehow sits back into the landscape and disappears.

NOTAMAN

What good is a rock going to do you?

READYMAID

I don't know, but it's more than I had before.

They look around them. The forest is dark and seems to stretch in every direction.

READYMAID

Where to, now?

They walk. The rustling of leaves beneath their feet, in the trees. They walk. More rustling. They walk. More rustling. They walk. More rustling. It gets louder and more consistent, and they stop.

NOTAMAN

(calling out) Is someone there?

Silence. They keep walking. More rustling of leaves. They stop again.

NOTAMAN

Who's there?

An owl hoots. They walk. More rustling. They stop moving and the rustling continues as if they're walking.

READYMAID

This rustling isn't really escalating at all. Maybe we should ignore it.

NOTAMAN

I think we should wait until it comes to a head.

More rustling. Then RUSSELL's head floats up out of the bushes. He is seen, but continues to focus on making rustling sounds, not noticing READYMAID or Notaman.

NOTAMAN

See?! I was right.

RUSSELL

(as he rustles) Rustle russell rustle Russell. Rustle Russell.

READYMAID

(gently trying to get his attention) Excuse me? Can you—

RUSSELL

Rustle russell rustle russell

NOTAMAN

Hey. Hey! What are you doing?

RUSSELL stops, looks up.

RUSSELL

What?

NOTAMAN

What are you doing rustling around down there?

RUSSELL

Oh sorry, is it making you uncomfortable?

READYMAID

It's just very suspicious is all. Being in a dark forest.

RUSSELL

Right. Well, I'm just doing foley.

READYMAID

Sorry, what does that mean?

RUSSELL

Foley. In the foliage. I'm creating textured sounds for your forest walk. You know, underbrush-swiping, dry leaves crunching, owl hooting.

An owl hoots.

READYMAID

And you do this for a living?

RUSSELL

Yeah.

READYMAID

Under whose employment?

RUSSELL

My own.

READYMAID

You're self-employed?

RUSSELL

Works for me. Whatever you want to call it.

READYMAID

I only ask because I'm on——

NOTAMAN hits her.

READYMAID

——maternity leave. From my job.

RUSSELL

(whatever) Right.

An owl hoots. Rustling.

READYMAID

Can I ask, is that your calling?

RUSSELL

Oh no, mine sounds like this. *(owl-like)* Hoo!

READYMAID

No, I mean, your higher purpose. Are you fulfilled?

RUSSELL

It's occasionally thankless. Just yesterday I made the sound of a tree falling, but no one was there to hear it.

READYMAID

Then did you really make the sound?

RUSSELL

Of course I did.

NOTAMAN

Okay, we'll just move along then, uh…sorry, what's your name?

RUSSELL

Russell.

NOTAMAN

Figures.

READYMAID

Okay, bye then. Come on, Notaman.

RUSSELL

Hey, wait a minute. I know about you guys.

READYMAID

Us?

RUSSELL

Sure, the art objects.

NOTAMAN

Who told you?

RUSSELL

Words echo fast in the forest.

READYMAID

I hope no one else heard.

RUSSELL

I heard you guys are headed to Wit's End.

NOTAMAN

We didn't say that.

READYMAID

We are?

RUSSELL

Wait, no...*(shaking head)* was I not supposed to say that? Oh, russell russell russell.

NOTAMAN

(to READYMAID) I don't think that's the sound of a head shaking. *(to RUSSELL)* Who told you we were headed to *(whisper)* Wit's End?

RUSSELL

I heard it through the grapevine.

NOTAMAN looks up and around at all the hanging forest vines.

NOTAMAN

Which one? I'll tear it down.

RUSSELL

That one.

RUSSELL points to a GRAPEVINE of three people dancing soberly through the trees, rather quickly.

NOTAMAN

Hey, stop!

The GRAPEVINE doesn't notice, keeps dancing its way through the trees.

NOTAMAN

Readymaid, let's go! That grapevine knows something!

READYMAID

(as they run off after it, fading into the distance) I bet it knows a lot. After all, it's an Ivy League!

NOTAMAN and READYMAID chase off after the GRAPEVINE. RUSSELL stares after them.

The chorus of Marvin Gaye's "Heard it through the Grapevine" plays as the stage shifts to show how quickly READYMAID and NOTAMAN are moving through the forest. We watch the GRAPEVINE elude them at every turn. Finally, they are out of breath and give in. The GRAPEVINE escapes.

Scene IV

A different part of the forest, later in the evening. An almost ultraviolet darkness. There is a fork in the road, which is a literal giant fork that has many signposts that points in many directions, with words in all-caps. We hear the buzzing sound from the hospital scene. Cicadas? The first thing we see is the GRAPEVINE of people moving very quickly across the stage and off.

READYMAID and NOTAMAN burst on, outchased, panting.

NOTAMAN

Clawfoot tub, they got away.

READYMAID looks around, taking in their new surroundings.

READYMAID

Notaman, does the Forest of Whimsy suddenly seem less... whimsical to you?

They both look around. It is very dark. READYMAID spots a literal giant fork standing in the road.

READYMAID

Well, you said to look for the signs. There are a lot here.

They approach the fork in the road.

NOTAMAN

I can't make them out in this light. Any of them say *(whisper)* "Wit's End?"

READYMAID

No.

NOTAMAN

How about just "The Capital?"

READYMAID

It's all capitals. Oh, I can't stand this.

NOTAMAN

You don't have to.

NOTAMAN poses like an ottoman.

NOTAMAN

I could be a surface.

READYMAID

That's not what I meant, but thank you.

Then, a disembodied voice—the SUBJUNCTIVE—is heard:

SUBJUNCTIVE

If I were you, I might go that a-way.

NOTAMAN gets up. They look around for the source of the voice, but see nothing.

NOTAMAN

Hey, who said that?

SUBJUNCTIVE

Or perhaps I should suggest you walk in that direction.

READYMAID

Where's it coming from?

SUBJUNCTIVE

Or perhaps I'd recommend you stay rooted right where you are, since you don't seem to to know where you're going. Keep one foot on the ground.

NOTAMAN

HEY, who you calling a futon? *(fisticuffs)*

READYMAID

Alright, wherever you are, come out. We're terribly lost!

SUBJUNCTIVE

Can't help you there. At least not from all the way over here.

READYMAID

Well, if we could see you...it's just that it's very dark out here...

SUBJUNCTIVE

How about now?

THE SUBJUNCTIVE sheds some light, revealing himself. He is dressed in the kind of costume that you might imagine a grammatical concept wearing. It includes a cape.

READYMAID

Oh, my. What...Who...What I mean is...

SUBJUNCTIVE

It isn't what you mean, but how you mean. Or rather, how I mean. I mean well, unless I were to...*(pause)* Better that you ask me to introduce myself.

READYMAID

Alright.

SUBJUNCTIVE

(bows) Subjunctive here. And you're at my subjunction. The intersection of pure furtherance, where the only way to move forward is by recommendation.

NOTAMAN

You're the subjunctive? *(pause)* Like the tense?

SUBJUNCTIVE

Actually I'm more of a mood. In tense. That is, I can only be seen in certain tenses. That's why I live here, in my mood lighting.

READYMAID

That's quite the introduction. What should we call you?

SUBJUNCTIVE

Jeff.

NOTAMAN

Jeff?

SUBJUNCTIVE

Yep.

READYMAID

Well, Jeff, my friend here and I are questing. Re-questing, really, since I'm living a double life. That is, living it over again.

SUBJUNCTIVE

I don't follow.

READYMAID

It's hard to explain. Let's put it this way: I was employed. But now I'm self-employed. A freelancer. And Notaman, here—

NOTAMAN

I can freely answer too, it's alright. I'm a daybed gone rogue. An ex-chaise. A footrest on sabbatical! *(pause)* I used to be a couch.

SUBJUNCTIVE

Ouch.

READYMAID

We each have recently discovered our inherent value not only as humans, but as works of art. And now, I think we are going to a place called *(whisper)* Wit's End. So if you could help us get there—

The SUBJUNCTIVE jumps at the words "Wit's End"
and is gone.

NOTAMAN

Where'd he go?

READYMAID

Hello? Jeff?

SUBJUNCTIVE's voice is heard from the trees:

SUBJUNCTIVE

Leave me alone.

READYMAID

Did we say something to offend you?

SUBJUNCTIVE

Go away.

READYMAID

We didn't mean to upset you. We're just trying to find our way to Wit's End.

SUBJUNCTIVE

Stop saying it!

NOTAMAN

Wit's End?

SUBJUNCTIVE

I'm never going back and I'm certainly not helping anyone get there.

READYMAID

You've been?

SUBJUNCTIVE

I escaped.

READYMAID

You were a prisoner?

SUBJUNCTIVE

In a manner of speaking. We were employed.

READYMAID

Reluctantly, I take it.

SUBJUNCTIVE

Against my will. I had to recommend how crimes against the -Archy should be punished.

READYMAID

Oh, dear.

SUBJUNCTIVE

One day I wasn't in the mood.

NOTAMAN

(grimacing) Oh, no.

SUBJUNCTIVE

I wasn't. I couldn't bring myself to make such awful suggestions, knowing they would be carried out.

NOTAMAN

What did you do?

SUBJUNCTIVE

Everything I could. I left hanging clauses. I amended statements so that my sentences couldn't function.

READYMAID

I'm sure they didn't take too kindly to insubordination.

SUBJUNCTIVE starts crying.

READYMAID

(softly) Did they punish you?

SUBJUNCTIVE

They killed my relatives.

READYMAID

Oh, Jeff.

SUBJUNCTIVE

Hypothetical. Conditional. Potential. All the moods that held the world's hopes and dreams, that indicated there could still be an unknown. Snuffed out. The only one they left alive was Imperative, made chief commander. And he told me to escape before they could found me.

READYMAID

(furious) They won't get away with this.

SUBJUNCTIVE

That was many years ago. I think. Living in so many different tenses confuses your sense of Time.

READYMAID

We're going to Wit's End.

SUBJUNCTIVE

What's the point?

READYMAID

There is no point.

She pulls out her rock.

READYMAID

But there's a purpose.

SUBJUNCTIVE

You can if you want to. I can never go back.

READYMAID

(with growing confidence) You can. You can come with us. And we're going to defeat the -Archy, one by one, until we nullify the suffix itself.

SUBJUNCTIVE

What makes you so sure you can?

READYMAID

Because they won't see me coming. I am Ready-made, an immaculate concept born to rend the Myth of Objectivity from the clutches of an -Archical world. So we will go to Wit's End, and we will fell the Towers of Reason, and distill unto all a New Era, one that is eternally up-to-date and thus beyond obsolescence. Down with the State of the Archy. And long live the State-of-the-Art!

NOTAMAN and SUBJUNCTIVE

Wow.

READYMAID

So you'll take us there, Jeff? You're one of us too, after all. Not a found art, but a lost one.

SUBJUNCTIVE

(beat) Oh, You'll like me. You'll like my company very much. I'm never insubordinate.

READYMAID

Excellent. Come along then! We'd better get a move on if we want to reach *(whisper)* Wit's End...

NOTAMAN, READYMAID and SUBJUNCTIVE
link arms and do that walk from The Wizard of Oz,
as the lights shift to a space we haven't seen before. We
can only assume that it's at Wit's End, inside the King's
chamber. FORM stares into a mirror that shows the
image of the three Art Objects en route.

FORM

Readymade is coming. And she found friends. *(He paces.)*
This calls for decisive action: a temporary stoppage.
Something to interrupt her mission.

FORM goes over to his bookcase and pulls a tome
down. He flips through the pages, scanning.

FORM

Let's see... hero's journey, hero's journey... hero, hero's
downfall, hero's duty... oh! here. *(He reaches a page and reads*
aloud.) "Hero's Journey: (n.) a quest of varying lengths of
time, usually episodic and relating to prophecy, slowed only
by the use of an external device. *(beat)* She already knows
about the Retrospect...*(reading)* external device (see also:
deus ex machina). *(He turns the pages.)* "Deus ex machina
(n.): An unexpected power or event saving a seemingly
hopeless situation, especially as a contrived plot device (see
also)." *(He turns the pages.)* "Plot device (n.): Anything
which moves the plot forward. *(Beat. Aside.)* But how can we
move it backward? *(Reading)* A contrived or arbitrary plot
device—yes!—may annoy or confuse—yes!—causing a loss
of the suspension of desbelief."

(beat) FORM grumbles. Mutters to himself. Thinks for
a while.

FORM

Oh, alright!

FORM gets up and opens a door, behind which DISBELIEF is sleeping hanging shackled by his wrists. When FORM opens the door, DISBELIEF starts awake and stares at FORM, who grumpily begins unshackling him.

FORM

You're free to go.

DISBELIEF

You can't be serious.

FORM

It's a small price to pay.

DISBELIEF

I can't believe it!

FORM

Shut up! I hate that! *(incoherent grumbling, then,)* A truant for a truism. A praxis for a proxy.

He finishes unshackling DISBELIEF, and is now simply holding him in the air by the wrist.

FORM

I hope I don't live to regret this.

He lets go.

As soon as \DISBELIEF's feet touch the ground, there is a blackout.

INTERMISSION

ACT II

Scene I

The sun rises on the Forest of Whimsy. READYMAID, NOTAMAN and SUBJUNCTIVE are standing in the same positions as before, frozen in place. In a moment they come to life, walking as before. Only READYMAID notices the strangeness of what just happened.

READYMAID

What an odd. Feeling I just had. Where..? I'm...

NOTAMAN

You okay, Readymaid?

READYMAID

(looking around her) I think so. I just lost my bearings. Morning already? *(beat)* That was awfully expedient. Didn't...didn't we set out just yesterday?

NOTAMAN

Yes...

SUBJUNCTIVE

I think you ought to sit down.

READYMAID steadies herself against a rock, begins to sit down.

NOTAMAN

(pointing) Watch out for that hard place.

She avoids it and sits, adjusting, adjusting. Cicadas. After a few moments:

READYMAID

I suppose it's true, what they say. Time flies when you're on a prophetic quest to defeat an all-powerful authority and simultaneously trying to understand your god-given purpose on earth.

NOTAMAN

Who says that?

READYMAID

You know. "They" do.

NOTAMAN

Who's they?

READYMAID

(thinking) That's interesting. I never really/

SUBJUNCTIVE

/The council.

READYMAID

(looking up) The council?

SUBJUNCTIVE

It's more of a congregation, really. The Forest's Aptest Council of Latter-Day Perpetual Tense. *(bitterly)* I wasn't allowed to join.

READYMAID

I'm sorry.

SUBJUNCTIVE

It's alright. I was planning to present my case for "Admit Tense" before the council, but. *(pause)* I just never got around to it. I'm not very driven.

READYMAID

And the council declares things like, "Time flies when you're on a prophetic quest to defeat an all-powerful authority and simultaneously trying to understand your god-given purpose on earth?"

SUBJUNCTIVE

So they say.

NOTAMAN

The more you know.

SUBJUNCTIVE

One can't be entirely certain, but no one cares much for proving or disproving who dwells in the Forest of Whimsy.

READYMAID

What about the -Archy?

SUBJUNCTIVE

Disapproving, maybe, but they don't bother much with us here.

The sound of a chainsaw. They all jump and look around themselves, but see nothing. NOTAMAN goes full table and screams. Furniture trauma, go figure.

The chainsaw stops. A brief silence. Then, a huge boom, the sound of a tree falling. They jump again.

NOTAMAN

Do you think it's Russell?

READYMAID

I'm not sure.

Another chainsaw sound, silence, and a tree falling.

READYMAID

It's coming from over there!

They all follow the sound into a clearing, where they discover the following scene: an official-looking person—The ARCHIVIST—with a clipboard, moving through the trees and taking notes. The ARCHIVIST stops in front of a tree, and takes notes. Then he nods to his henchman, MUSCLE, who cuts down the tree with a chainsaw.

NOTAMAN

Hey! You!

ARCHIVIST glances up at the group briefly, then goes back to his task.

NOTAMAN

Hey! HEY!

READYMAID

Excuse me!

When ARCHIVIST hears READYMAID's voice, he stops and looks up. So does Muscle.

NOTAMAN

Hey, Russell!

MUSCLE

Uh. Muscle. You mean Russell, my twin brother?

READYMAID

Your twin...yes, if it's the same Russell we met yesterday, on our way to—

NOTAMAN hits her.

READYMAID

—uesday. On our way, Tuesday.

MUSCLE

(suspiciously) Yesterday was Friday.

READYMAID

(recovering) Well yes, I meant, on our way to Tuesday. We're just walking until we reach next week. *(pause)* It's a very expedient way to time-travel.

MUSCLE

Right.

Beat. She looks at the trees, many of which have been cut down. SUBJUNCTIVE is also looking, stricken.

READYMAID

May I ask what you're doing, cutting down all these trees?

ARCHIVIST

They're of no use anymore. Now that they're in here.

He gestures to his clipboard.

NOTAMAN

What's that?

ARCHIVIST

Archives. I'm an Archivist.

NOTAMAN

Never heard of that job.

ARCHIVIST

You know cemeteries?

NOTAMAN

What about cemeteries?

ARCHIVIST

That's me.

READYMAID

Archives? But these are trees.

ARCHIVIST

Yes, so?

READYMAID

There's no reason to archive trees.

ARCHIVIST

There most certainly is a reason. Just because they don't speak or vote or make jokes

SUBJUNCTIVE

Trees make jokes/

ARCHIVIST

/or choose between dinner options or lie down and get back up or pay taxes or put dogs on leashes or open doors or give birth to other trees

SUBJUNCTIVE

Trees make trees/

ARCHIVIST

/or go to hospitals when they're sick or get college degrees or write novels/

SUBJUNCTIVE

Trees write plays/

ARCHIVIST

/or emigrate to other forests or run out of things to say to someone they wish they weren't talking to, that doesn't excuse them from census. Even nature can be arranged. Should be arranged.

SUBJUNCTIVE

Shouldn't you arrange it with the people who live in the forest, before you go destroying it?

ARCHIVIST

Don't need to ask. On orders from the Archy.

ARCHIVIST pulls out a sign that says FOREST OF WHIMSY: GROUNDS FOR REMOVAL.

SUBJUNCTIVE

The -Archy! *(beat)* But what are they putting in its place?

ARCHIVIST

Just deserts, I think. But I don't ask questions. *(beat)* Say, aren't you the art objects?

NOTAMAN

Who wants to know?

ARCHIVIST

I do.

NOTAMAN

On orders from the Archy?

ARCHIVIST pulls out a sign that says WANDERING STRANGERS: GROUNDS FOR SUSPICION.

READYMAID

Well, if you must know/

NOTAMAN hits her.

READYMAID

Notaman! I'm—

NOTAMAN

—We're just passing through. There's no reason to be suspicious of us.

ARCHIVIST

There most certainly is a Reason. You're not. on any of my lists. You haven't been accounted for.

NOTAMAN

We'll spare you the trouble. One, two, three. There.

ARCHIVIST

I'm afraid I'll have to ask you to come to your census.

MUSCLE takes a threatening step toward them with the chainsaw.

READYMAID

That's nonsense.

ARCHIVIST

That's insulting.

READYMAID

Notes on a clipboard aren't a replacement for people.

ARCHIVIST

Certainly it does. People get replaced the day they're born. What's your name?

NOTAMAN

Nevermind what her name is!

ARCHIVIST

Testy, testy. Just trying to prove a point. *(beat)* And I already know your name.

SUBJUNCTIVE

We should be going now.

READYMAID

What's the purpose of an archive if the thing it points to no longer exists?

ARCHIVIST

Order, for one.

READYMAID

But that only keeps the past in order.

ARCHIVIST

Correction. It keeps the future in order.

READYMAID

Not if someone using it doesn't know we existed.

ARCHIVIST

Ridiculous. They'd know you existed. That's what the archives are for. They provide an irrefutably accurate record of life as it was.

READYMAID

No, they don't.

ARCHIVIST

(interested) What do you mean?

READYMAID

Your archive only provides a record of me the moment before you did away with me, *(she gestures at the fallen trees),* a moment with fallen trees. It doesn't include the record of me before the trees fell.

ARCHIVIST

I'll add it, then. Now.

He scribbles.

MUSCLE takes another step.

READYMAID

Or yesterday, when I didn't have a rock in my pocket.

ARCHIVIST scribbles quickly.

NOTAMAN

Or me when I was on all fours.

SUBJUNCTIVE

Or me when I had more hair.

ARCHIVIST

(attempting to scribble) Slow down! I'm writing.

NOTAMAN

Testy, testy.

SUBJUNCTIVE

We're only trying to prove a point.

The ARCHIVIST looks up.

READYMAID

If you really wanted to keep a complete record of life as it was in every moment, you wouldn't destroy the things you put on your clipboard.

ARCHIVIST

What do you mean? That would make me a terrible Archivist.

READYMAID

Not at all. You'd be the most important Archivist there ever was in the -Archy.

ARCHIVIST

How?

READYMAID

You'd invent the first living archive, an eternal record that never went out of date.

Silence. MUSCLE looks at the ARCHIVIST expectantly.

ARCHIVIST

   (beat) Where would I start?

READYMAID

   Start with us.

NOTAMAN

   Readymaid!

READYMAID

   You can take as many notes as you need, we'll wait here and tell you anything you like.

SUBJUNCTIVE

   Readymaid!

READYMAID

   Only afterwards, instead of doing away with us, you could let us pass.

ARCHIVIST

   (pause) I'd be out of a job.

READYMAID

   You could archive it.

   The ARCHIVIST pauses, considering. After a moment, he begins scribbling.

   Blackout.

Scene II

The lights come up on another part of the forest.
READYMAID, SUBJUNCTIVE and NOTAMAN
are still traveling. The day is waning.

NOTAMAN

Readymaid, you've got to stop giving us away.

SUBJUNCTIVE

For all we know, no one but everyone we've met so far
knows that we're headed to *(whisper)* Wit's End.

READYMAID

I know. But ever since I found my purpose I've had a
strange predilection for telling the Truth.

NOTAMAN

The Truth isn't going to get us to the -Archy. Not alive,
anyway.

READYMAID

It might. The Archivist said he didn't know how we were
going to get to *(whisper)* Wit's End. Why wouldn't he
know? From the sounds of it, he had every corner of the
forest mapped out.

NOTAMAN

Maybe he didn't want to tell us. He obviously knew who
we were.

SUBJUNCTIVE

Because it's not on a map.

NOTAMAN

Then how do you know which way we're going?

SUBJUNCTIVE

I don't. At least, topographically speaking.

NOTAMAN

WHAT? We've been walking for days.

SUBJUNCTIVE

This is the way.

NOTAMAN

How could you possibly know?

READYMAID

Jeff's right, Notaman. Befortune said Form "found" *(whisper)* Wit's End. What if, in order to find it, we have to go mad?

SUBJUNCTIVE nods soberly.

SUBJUNCTIVE

I told you I didn't want to go back.

NOTAMAN

But how would we do that?

SUBJUNCTIVE

I'm not quite sure. I suppose we'll just cross that bridge when we come to it.

NOTAMAN

Hey look! A bridge! Looks like a shortcut!

Notaman is pointing at a bridge that seems to connect two disparate parts of the forest. They stand at the foot of the bridge. It looks treacherous. SUBJUNCTIVE is visibly apprehensive.

SUBJUNCTIVE

I suggest that we/

NOTAMAN

/We should take it!

READYMAID

Shouldn't we stick to the path? I don't know that I trust a bridged version of it.

NOTAMAN

You just said we should cross a bridge if we see one,/

READYMAID

That's not quite what I/

NOTAMAN

/and besides. If there's one thing I've learned from being a piece of furniture, it's that you should always trust the slats.

READYMAID

But what if this skips us right over something important?

NOTAMAN

Oh, come on. We've been skipping the entire time! Why stop now?

NOTAMAN puts a foot out onto the bridge.

NOTAMAN

Whoa.

He steadies himself.

READYMAID

Notaman, I—

READYMAID catches sight of a journal lying on the forest floor. She reads the monogram aloud: "M.P.R.S.S.M."

NOTAMAN looks over at READYMAID, who has opened the journal and is beginning to read.

READYMAID

"2:30pm. Readymaid, Notaman and the Subjunctive join together and travel through the Forest of Whimsy to reach the capital city. 3:30pm They stop for lunch. 4:00pm Notaman relieves himself behind a tree. 4:15pm The tree re-leaves itself."

NOTAMAN

That all sounds awfully familiar.

READYMAID

That's because it's exactly what we were doing. Right on schedule, down to a T. *(She keeps reading.)* 4:30pm They play golf. 4:45pm They set off again through the poplar field. The Subjunctive suggests a different route, but is downvoted by poplar opinion.

SUBJUNCTIVE

(bitterly) I recommended that we stay overnight at the inn. Then we could have taken the inn field.

NOTAMAN

(offended) Out of left-field, Jeff! We voted on it!

READYMAID

These are field notes…about us!

READYMAID looks around, and spies a binder on the ground. She opens it in such a way that the audience can see that there are binder tabs. She gasps.

READYMAID

Someone's been keeping tabs on us!

They gasp. JEFF turns around and scoots his cape over. Anyway, there's a reveal that he has a large letter I taped to his back. He gasps.

SUBJUNCTIVE

They've had an I on me this entire time!

NOTAMAN steps off the bridge and rolls up his sleeve.
He realizes he's wearing a watch. He gasps.

NOTAMAN

We're being watched!

SUBJUNCTIVE

It's not safe here. Let's go this way!

He gestures to an area of the forest that is particularly
untouched and scary-looking.

SUBJUNCTIVE

They won't be able to follow us.

SUBJUNCTIVE starts to go. Noticing that no one is
following him, he turns back.

SUBJUNCTIVE

For once, can we all just take my advice?

He grumbles ad libs of "This is my only purpose on
earth" as they follow him. Lights fade as NOTAMAN,
READYMAID and the SUBJUNCTIVE link arms
and head into the forest.

ACT III
Scene I

The Forest of Whimsy. The sun is high and the scene is beautifully lit, almost celestial in beauty. READYMAID, SUBJUNCTIVE AND JEFF have been walking for a long time. They are very tired. It is evening again, or the next day. Their skipping and cavorting gait from earlier has flagged, and is now just a slow lope.

NOTAMAN

When does it end?

SUBJUNCTIVE

When we go insane.

READYMAID

I think I've seen this tree before.

NOTAMAN

You know what they say.

READYMAID

It does seem as though we're going in circles.

SUBJUNCTIVE

The -Archy wouldn't dare make something so infinite.

NOTAMAN

My legs hurt, (he grips his legs), and I'm so hungry. I've never been this hungry before. I always just ate the crumbs that fell when people sat on me.

READYMAID

And yet, it still feels like we're just a stone's throw away. Oh!

READYMAID remembers the stone in her pocket. She picks it up and throws it. It hits a tree. A plum falls.

READYMAID

Hm. Somehow, I thought that would work.

Another plum falls.

I know signs don't grow on trees, but I do wish/

A plum falls.

/we'd get some sort of…I don't know, indication that we were progressing, or/

A plum falls.

/just that our environment might start to reflect the gravity of the situation.

A bushel of plums tumbles down behind them. NOTAMAN jumps and turns around, but when he sees what it is, he becomes jovial.

NOTAMAN

Plums!

READYMAID looks up and around.

READYMAID

It's an orchard!

NOTAMAN

Look at all this low-hanging fruit!

NOTAMAN goes to pick a plum from a nearby branch but SUBJUNCTIVE stops him.

SUBJUNCTIVE

I wouldn't. We don't know whether they're safe to eat.

NOTAMAN begrudgingly drops the fruit as they continue walking, scowling at SUBJUNCTIVE. A dog is barking up one of the trees as they pass.

SUBJUNCTIVE

And we can't see through all these trees. Maybe we ought to turn back and take the bridge.

NOTAMAN

Oh, now you want to take the bridge? But when I wanted/ to

SUBJUNCTIVE

I didn't say that we should take the bridge, I just/ think we should assess

NOTAMAN

You know, I've really had it with all your nagging/ recommendations about this and that, which way to go

SUBJUNCTIVE

Nagging? Well, maybe I've had it with all your emotional baggage/ about being a piece of furniture

NOTAMAN

Baggage? I'll show you baggage, you one-use sorry *(fisticuffs)* excuse for a sentence structure/

READYMAID

Boys! What are you fighting about? *(beat)* Isn't that odd? I've suddenly got the strangest sense of déjà-vu...

From up in a tree, the MNEMONIST jumps down, surprising them all. He has a charming twinkle in his eye, but his tone is sinister.

MNEMONIST

Look alive!

READYMAID

Oh!

NOTAMAN

I do so!

JEFF

Why, I oughta…

MNEMONIST

Are you folks lost?

READYMAID

No, we were just—

She catches herself before NOTAMAN can.

READYMAID

—passing through. Sorry, I hope we're not intruding.

MNEMONIST

Not at all. In fact, I'd say you were on your way here all along.

READYMAID

We were?

MNEMONIST

Sure!

READYMAID

And here is…where, exactly?

MNEMONIST

This? Why, this is Fruition. A humble orchard where everything desired is finally attained.

READYMAID

I recognize you from somewhere.

MNEMONIST

Plum? The fruits of my labor for the fruit of yours *(he winks)*.

NOTAMAN

Yes, please!

NOTAMAN snatches the plum from MNEMONIST'S hands and bites, glowering smugly at SUBJUNCTIVE.

READYMAID

But I can't place you.

MNEMONIST

That follows.

READYMAID

Follows what?

MNEMONIST

Well, let's just say I don't quite stay put. Though I do stand in place.

READYMAID

Of?

MNEMONIST

Other things. People. Wherever I'm needed.

READYMAID

I can't...remember...

MNEMONIST

Sounds like you might need me, after all.

READYMAID

(gasps) it's you. You were my...but you look different.

MNEMONIST

The -Archy's mnemonist, at your service.

READYMAID

I was your...I was working for...you? How did you...? My whole life...

MNEMONIST

Part of on my power. I take names, nest in shapes, over and over, dividing to conquer.

READYMAID

I don't understand.

NOTAMAN, who has finished the fruit, now begins to stumble.

NOTAMAN

I feel funny.

He falls to the ground, unconscious.

READYMAID

Notaman!

SUBJUNCTIVE

Oh, I told him so!

MNEMONIST

(glancing at NOTAMAN) Whoops. Those things are ripe. *(He turns back to READYMAID.)* You know, I'd love to stick around for a walk down memory lane, Ready, but I'm actually here on business.

MNEMONIST quickly makes NOTAMAN and SUBJUNCTIVE disappear into the landscape. They are gone. READYMAID is horrified.

READYMAID

What have you done with them?

MNEMONIST

Confidential business, actually. Can't really discuss it.

The MNEMONIST snaps again and he, too, is gone.

READYMAID looks around her as the lights fade from friendly to ominous, the trees dying and fruit shriveling.

READYMAID

This wasn't a place called Fruition at all. Just some kind of illusion. A trick.

MNEMONIST'S VOICE

It's like you said earlier to a friend of mine, Readymaid. It's a living record. It's just not yours.

The MNEMONIST is gone. READYMAID is alone. In the mnemonist's place stands a mirror.

READYMAID walks over to the mirror and looks at herself (HERSELF). She tears up as she contemplates her reflection.

READYMAID

Who are you?

She traces her face in the mirror. She begins to cry. Her mirror image does not cry.

HERSELF

Why are you crying?

READYMAID jumps back, alarmed, having heard her own voice. She looks around her, expecting to see someone, but no one is there. She looks at the mirror.

READYMAID

Did I just—I didn't, did I?

She approaches the mirror once more and stares at HERSELF cautiously, regarding her reflection.

READYMAID

I think I'm having déja-vu.

HERSELF

French made —

READYMAID jumps.

HERSELF

—just like you.

READYMAID approaches the mirror and knocks twice to confirm it is solid.

HERSELF

Who's there?

READYMAID

Readymaid.

HERSELF

Readymaid who?

READYMAID

I don't know.

HERSELF

That's not funny.

READYMAID

I wasn't trying to be.

HERSELF

You could've. I've al-Readymaid my point, for example.

READYMAID

I don't have a point.

HERSELF

That's funny!

READYMAID

Why?

HERSELF

Because it's true.

READYMAID

At my expense.

HERSELF

Observations always come at someone's expense. No such thing as a free hunch.

READYMAID

(to herself) Am I talking to myself?

HERSELF

That depends on who you think I am.

READYMAID

I'm seeing someone.

HERSELF

At your service. Step into my office.

READYMAID

Me?

HERSELF

Aye.

READYMAID

An aye for an I.

HERSELF

A troth for a truth.

READYMAID

What truth?

HERSELF

It's self-evident.

READYMAID

Not to me.

HERSELF

To me, then.

READYMAID

I see only myself.

HERSELF

Look harder.

READYMAID

I don't know how.

HERSELF

Seeing is believing.

READYMAID

Looks can be deceiving.

HERSELF

Not where art is concerned.

READYMAID

But I was the deceiver. I'm not what people say I am.

HERSELF

Of course you aren't.

READYMAID

And that makes me a counterfeit.

HERSELF

You didn't make a claim.

READYMAID

But I don't want acclaim.

HERSELF

You'd rather be obscured?

READYMAID

I'd settle for cured. Curated, even. I could forgo an aesthetic.

HERSELF

Forgone, and thus forgotten. Is that what you want? To become obsolete?

READYMAID

I want to serve a purpose.

HERSELF

No greater than the sum of its parts.

READYMAID

But part of a whole, at least.

HERSELF

You'd rather belong than be wrong.

READYMAID

I had it maid.

HERSELF

You misheard. Happens to the best of us.

READYMAID

But I can't adhere.

HERSELF

Aren't you stuck now?

READYMAID does not respond. She is on the brink of madness.

HERSELF

There's only way to come unglued, Readymaid. Look inside yourself. Step into my orifice.

READYMAID approaches the mirror. She steps into it. Buzzing begins. Cicadas. It grows. It is deafening. Blackout.

Scene II

The lights come up dimly on a desolate, barren terminus. A sign at the entrance that reads "WIT'S END." The Forest of Whimsy is in the distance, a vestige of greenery; but we are beyond it now.

The sky is dusky, overcast. The sound of cicadas and crows.

READYMAID stands just beyond the gate. She has made it to Wit's End. She looks around and realizes this, amazed. She steps through a door into a grand marbled hall. No one is inside.

Within moments, however, members of the -Archy emerge: FORM, REASON, THE DEVIL, MUSCLE, THE EULOGIST. SUBJUNCTIVE and NOTAMAN wheeled out in shackles.

READYMAID

Notaman! Jeff!

NOTAMAN

It's okay, Readymaid. This is surprisingly familiar territory.

JEFF

Ditto.

KING FORM

I didn't think you had it in you, Readymaid.

READYMAID

Why not? I think I've been very consistent.

KING FORM

Persistent, at least. But you know what this means.

READYMAID

I don't think I ought to.

KING FORM

You were out of options. Hopeless. Destitute. You can't get to Wit's End without being at the end of your rope.

READYMAID

And this is the -Archy, I presume?

KING FORM

Our reputation precedes us.

READYMAID

I haven't had the pleasure. And I doubt I will, but feel free to introduce yourselves.

KING FORM

Certainly. His Majesty, King Form.

She looks to the EULOGIST.

READYMAID

And you. I know you already.

EULOGIST

Readymaid, I'm—

READYMAID

I can't even look at you. And you?

DEVIL

I'm just the Devil. *(smooth)* Come on, you knew I'd be here.

READYMAID

And you. The -Arch's Mnemonist.

MNEMONIST

Your second opinion, friendly neighborhood stand-in. A if you will.

READYMAID

(automatically) Alternatives to the word alternative. *(pause)* Sorry, reflex. *(pause)* In Retrospect...

KING FORM

(gesturing to MNEMONIST) A simple mnemonic device, Readymaid. You understand.

MNEMONIST

(winking) We're still testing it. I was afraid we'd have to recall them.

DEVIL

I wanted to call it a demonic device, but no.

READYMAID

All this time I haven't known whether we were running away from you or towards you. But it didn't matter.

She looks at the EULOGIST.

READYMAID

It was all predetermined.

SUBJUNCTIVE

It wasn't, Readymaid, they made me make suggestions...!

KING FORM

Quiet! We didn't take any of them. A pleasantly logical conclusion you've come to, Readymaid. You'd never have found your way here with all that wishy-washy intuiting. And we couldn't summon you to Wit's End without Reason.

REASON

(from offstage) Accounted for!

REASON enters, excitedly. She is MISS SIEVE from ACT I. READYMAID sees REASON, and recognizes her as her former employer.

READYMAID

Miss Sieve?

REASON

(coyly) You must have me confused with someone else. I'm Reason.

READYMAID

No, I'm certain it's you. You don't remember me? Readymaid?

REASON

Doesn't ring a bell.

READYMAID

But you did.

Beat. She looks at the EULOGIST

READYMAID

And so did you. *(She looks at each of the members of the -Archy.)* And you. And you. And you.

DEVIL

The hell I did.

KING FORM

Come now, Readymaid, listen to Reason. She was listening to you, after all.

KING FORM holds up the field notes.

REASON

Forgive me for doing it all by hand, sometimes I'm such a luddite.

READYMAID

M.P.R.S.S.M.? Forgive me, I didn't recognize you initially.

REASON

Those aren't my initials. They're yours.

READYMAID

Mine!

REASON

Yes. *(beat)* I'm not going to spell it out for you. I took your journal from the guesthouse, I needed something to write on.

READYMAID looks pleadingly at the EULOGIST, her heart breaking.

READYMAID

Am I not a Messiah?

KING FORM

A messiah! You're just a piece of junk somebody decided to call a work of art. A cheap excuse to make a prophet.

READYMAID

(cold) I misheard.

NOTAMAN

Don't listen to him, Readymaid!

KING FORM

You're already-made. Commonplace. Out of date. Happens to everybody.

READYMAID

What do you want from me?

KING FORM

It's what we don't want from you. Dissent, for one.

READYMAID

We can't agree to disagree?

(beat) READYMAID is suddenly having déja-vu.

KING FORM

We deal in absolutes. You're either for us, or—

READYMAID

I've been here before.

KING FORM

What?

READYMAID looks around her, regarding.

READYMAID

That's why I can never add "here." It's been here all along, in the back of my mind. An afterthought trapped in my past that I couldn't see without hindsight.

READYMAID looks at the EULOGIST. He nods.

KING FORM

Don't be silly, Readymaid. I think we'd have taken notice.

READYMAID

You did. When you made me.

KING FORM

Made you! *(laughing)* Do you hear this?

EULOGIST

Give in, Form. She knows.

KING FORM

I will NOT GIVE IN. There's nothing to know.

READYMAID

I'm sure you blocked it out, with everything else. Squared the truth away in some corner of your kingdom where you never had to reckon with it. But I could see it in your "I's."

READYMAID walks over to SUBJUNCTIVE and pulls the I off of his back.

READYMAID

We have the same handwriting. You may not have been ready when you made me but I am Ready-made, an immaculate concept born to rend the Myth of Objectivity from the clutches of an -Archical world. And I'm here to end your reign, by any means necessary. Whatever that means. Maybe. Whatever that means may be.

KING FORM is apoplectic.

KING FORM

ENOUGH!

KING FORM signals his henchmen.

KING FORM

Take her away. *(beat)* Put her in the room with no way out.

Henchmen grab READYMAID and begin taking her offstage. She resists, to little avail.

KING FORM

You think you know Wit's End, Readymaid. You think you've been here before. We'll just see how well. When your mind goes, here, it's not Wit you lose. It's your life.

The EULOGIST is distraught. READYMAID is taken out. Everylone looks at each other.

KING FORM

I think that went well. Or should I say—

Throughout this scene, the SUBJUNCTIVE has been getting angrier and angrier. In measured breaths, with growing intensity:

SUBJUNCTIVE

You. Shouldn't. Say. You. Shouldn't. Say. Anything. I'm the
only one. Who gets. To make. SUGGESTIONS!

*SUBJUNCTIVE breaks out of his shackles and rushes
to FOrm. They grapple. REASON screams. With
some effort, MNEMONIST and DEVIL rush to pull
SUBJUNCTIVE off of him. FORM dusts himself off
as the SUBJUNCTIVE thrashes in their grip.*

KING FORM

That wasn't wise, JEFF

SUBJUNCTIVE

I never claimed to be.

KING FORM

I didn't think you'd come back, after last time.

SUBJUNCTIVE

Neither did I. But meeting a Messiah changes things.

KING FORM

You know I was saving your brother, out of charity. But do
you what he said when he saw you coming? *(pause)* He said
"Kill him."

SUBJUNCTIVE

I don't believe you.

KING FORM

It doesn't matter whether you do or don't, frankly. We did
away with Disbelief a long time ago.

KING FORM gives a signal and swiftly, without laying a finger on him, the MNEMONIST re-arranges SUBJUNCTIVE's internal organs, renaming them after one another until they are utterly mutilated. It is torturous. THE SUBJUNCTIVE crumples.

NOTAMAN

JEFF! What happened?

EULOGIST

(in despair) What did you think would happen? We're at Wit's End. Language is always the first to go.

The -Archy is still. From his shackles, through tears:

NOTAMAN

It's alright, JEFF. It's going to be alright.

SUBJUNCTIVE

(fading) I see...my mood lighting...it's almost white...

NOTAMAN

(through tears) No! Come away from the mood lighting! Stay here, in the present!

The SUBJUNCTIVE is fading.

SUBJUNCTIVE

If only I were more than a cautionary mood, living on borrowed tense. A figure of a man caught up in a figurative manner of speaking. Imprisoned in first-person, with conjugal visits from my relatives. I guess some part of me thought I would live on to infinitive. To BE! Or...not to be. *(weakly)* Prose-blood.

He dies. NOTAMAN wails.

KING FORM

Oh, chin up. he didn't need our help.

THE DEVIL

He was already dying.

KING FORM

The last of his kind.

REASON

I never understood him, anyway.

KING FORM turns to the EULOGIST

KING FORM

Do you have something prepared?

The EULOGIST steps forward. He looks up and out, at everyone who stands waiting, expectantly, for his delivery.

EULOGIST

I'm speechless.

KING FORM

Speechless? That's impossible.

The Subjunctive wheezes out a posthumous breath.

SUBJUNCTIVE

May I suggest…this…

He is dead.

EULOGIST opens the slip of paper SUBJUNCTIVE has handed him, and begins to read aloud:

EULOGIST

Thank you all for gathering today. We are at a loss for words. The Subjunctive was a brave mood. Misunderstood, but always there to lend admonishment. Astonishing to those who knew him. He frustrated all of friends and obfuscated his enemies. Jeff is survived by his companions, Readymaid and Notaman, fellow works of art. Jeff's body of work will be scattered afield/

KING FORM

/That's enough./

EULOGIST

/in the forest where Jeff made his bed, yea, and lay in it. Among the grape-vines and ivies far from Wit's End/

KING FORM

/Stop./

EULOGIST

(emboldened) /So as not to feel tethered to our category. And there, let his plot thicken/

KING FORM

/I said stop!/

EULOGIST

/without periphery. For it is said that in the great "beyond", dead languages earn their wings. And—

KING FORM

(with deafening volume) SILENCE!

Everything falls silent except for the cicadas.

KING FORM

I said a speech, not a requiem.

REASON

It's disgusting. Who ever came up with the notion of someone sentimentalizing death for the living.

DEVIL

I did.

MNEMONIST

Speak of the Devil

DEVIL

Remember? We were having a meeting, and I said "Hey, we should have a person who goes around making people think that Death is this big ceremonial thing where you grieve and wear black and stuff, so more people fuck their lives up trying to escape it and then end up in hell with me," and you guys were like "Yeah, that sounds good."

MNEMONIST

I do remember that.

REASON

Perhaps I advocated for it at the time, but now look where it's got us. We've had someone on the inside working against us this entire time.

KING FORM

That's true. *(to EULOGIST)* Eul, it's clear your allegiance is elsewhere.

EULOGIST

Sir/

KING FORM

/I'm not sure how you tampered with the Retrospect, but—

EULOGIST

I didn't.

KING FORM

Oh? Then little theory about how did Readymaid arrive at this Wit's End?

EULOGIST

You really don't remember.

KING FORM

Not this again. Not the "I gave birth to found art" argument. It has no basis. No bearing.

EULOGIST

Only because you banished the woman who bore it.

KING FORM

Function was getting in the way.

EULOGIST

You were so busy making yourself a rule, you didn't know you'd conceived an exception.

KING FORM

No.

EULOGIST

Two, *(looks at REASON)* but one decided to follow you.

KING FORM

Everyone out. OUT. GET OUT!

Everyone exits but FORM. He lets out a yell that shakes the foundations of his castle and shatters the lights. Blackout.

Scene III

The room with no way out. Presumably somewhere in the basement of KING FORM's castle with no windows or doors or mirrors. It should feel coffin-like, impenetrable. Perhaps pitch-black. READYMAID stands motionless. The silence is deafening.

READYMAID

What a cliché. Found art in a negative space.

She looks around her. She cannot see anything.

READYMAID

It's certainly a sight for sore eyes. *(pause)* More of a blind spot, really. What's the use in talking aloud? To keep myself company, I suppose. To keep myself from feeling the time pass. I don't want to think about it! *(pause)* But I'll have to eventually. There's no way out.

PRESENCE

You know what we say.

READYMAID jumps.

READYMAID

Who said that?

PRESENCE

Does it really still surprise you to hear new voices, Readymaid?

READYMAID

You know my/

PRESENCE

Or that your name is known by everyone who crosses your path?

READYMAID

I assumed I was gaining some celebrity, but—

PRESENCE

Or that you manage to escape from even dire straits?

READYMAID

This one seems like a hard line.

PRESENCE

It isn't. You're impossible to apprehend, Readymaid. Others may attempt to stop you, but you are the only one with the power to arrest.

READYMAID

Maybe I should give it a rest.

PRESENCE

If I were you, I'd never stop.

READYMAID

And you are…?

PRESENCE

I am now. And now. And now.

READYMAID

And now?

PRESENCE

Yes.

READYMAID

Are you a part of the Council?

PRESENCE

I am.

READYMAID

The one Jeff wasn't allowed to join.

PRESENCE

He's more of a mood.

READYMAID

And you don't accept moods.

PRESENCE

I'm not sure if that's still the case. I've been down here a long time.

READYMAID

Did the -Archy put you here?

PRESENCE

I found my own way.

READYMAID

You got into a room with no way out?

PRESENCE

So did you.

READYMAID

That's true.

PRESENCE

And anyway, I'm not all here. Not entirely.

READYMAID

Where's the rest of you?

PRESENCE

Everywhere.

READYMAID

Omnipresent?

PRESENCE

Comes with the territory of perpetual tense. I'd rather this than Omni-past.

READYMAID

I didn't know there was such a thing.

PRESENCE

It's very unpleasant. He says it's like walking through mud. And he's always the last to know.

READYMAID

So you're everywhere.

PRESENCE

Where they'll have me. Some people can't bear it. Including the -Archy. This is as close as I can get.

READYMAID

What's that like?

PRESENCE

What?

READYMAID

To feel everywhere all at once?

PRESENCE

It's like having one hand on fire and the other in ice. It's like white hot hurt pouring through your insides. It's like looking up at the sky and realizing you're standing on your head.

READYMAID

I thought that's what this would feel like.

PRESENCE

What?

READYMAID

Purpose. I thought I had one.

PRESENCE

You don't.

READYMAID

I know.

PRESENCE

You don't have to have a purpose to serve one.

READYMAID

I used to work in service.

PRESENCE

That was different.

READYMAID

Seems the same to me.

PRESENCE

You have a curious tendency, Readymaid, to make two things one in your mind.

READYMAID

I can't help it.

PRESENCE

The greatest illusion is elision. Things that seem to go together, but don't. *(pause)* When really, they don't need to go together at all. *(pause)* Have you ever tried it the other way around?

READYMAID

I'm not sure I know what you mean.

PRESENCE

To split one thing in two. You might find it more helpful. Instead of talking your way into a room with no windows or doors, you could find a way out of it.

READYMAID

I can't begin to imagine. I can't even see in here.

PRESENCE

If it helps, I can offer a purpose. You could bring me with you.

READYMAID

Aren't you stuck down here?

PRESENCE

Not if you find us a way out.

READYMAID looks around her. It is pitch, pitch black and she cannot see PRESENCE.

READYMAID

I'm blind as a bat in here. *(beat)* I remember a riddle like this, once. About a man in a room with no windows or doors.

PRESENCE

How did it end?

READYMAID

He got out.

PRESENCE

Do you remember how?

READYMAID

(thinking) I can't remember.

PRESENCE

Split the thought. Split the thought in two.

READYMAID

I—

READYMAID grits her teeth, trying, trying.

PRESENCE

Halve it to hold it.

In the dark, we hear READYMAID crying and yelling as she tries. She suddenly sounds as if she's going into labor.

READYMAID

Can't…won't…couldn't…AHH!

PRESENCE

Deliver us, READYMAID

Suddenly, silence. A whooshing sound, as if someone is swinging a bat.

READYMAID

Let's go.

A whooshing sound.

PRESENCE

Wait! I can't go on my own. Carry me.

READYMAID picks PRESENCE up. She swings a bat. Once. Twice. Three times.

Scene IV

The grand hall of Wit's End. KING FORM is still pacing furiously. Perhaps days have passed since he began. Suddenly, he slows. He stops.

KING FORM

That's odd. I'm having a strange feeling. As if I've suddenly entered the room. But I'm here. I'm already here.

KING FORM holds his tightening chest. READYMAID enters, carrying PRESENCE. PRESENCE is a tiny thing, but she radiates.

READYMAID

I brought you a present.

KING FORM whirls around. READYMAID is advancing on him steadily, PRESENCE in her arms.

KING FORM

How did you—?

READYMAID

You think Wit's End is the purest achievement of Common Sense, when really it's the other way around. This is a common nonsense, a collective madness.

KING FORM

I made you.

KING FORM is backing up.

READYMAID

All it took was a new thought. My own.

KING FORM

I made you.

READYMAID

And I, you. You made me in your image: you stepped into the mirror, and I became your reflection. And I will stare back at you for as long as you live.

KING FORM begins to run to the door.

READYMAID

There's nowhere to hide. Your gates are open to interpretation. And the judgment of your crimes will be subjective.

KING FORM

You can't kill me. I am the rule that always applies!

READYMAID

Your rule is conditional. *(beat)* And I know your condition.

KING FORM

Name it.

READYMAID

Cardiac arrest.

KING FORM doubles over, his chest exploding with pure PRESENCE. He bleeds from every orifice. READYMAID watches, stony-faced.

READYMAID

And I, too, am an -Archy. Anarchy. It's innate. In nature, even. The heart begins in the right place, but somewhere along the way, we take a sharp left. I would have been content never to know you. But you questioned my purpose when I didn't have one. You tried to appraise me, but it only raised me to make you suffer. For as long as Form wears the crown and Reason is his concubine, art—TRUE, ART—must behave like the thing it dreads the most.

The bloody scene fades. From the rafters, DISBELIEF comes down. He is on a fly system, like Peter Pan. He inches ever so slightly toward the ground with every second, so that as he nears the end of this monologue his feet almost, almost touch ground. A black curtain falls over the stage in time with him.

DISBELIEF

Surprised to see me? Incredulous, even? The plot of this play took a turn, but I don't need to tell you which way it went. I'm just here to close up shop, make it easier for you to leave. After all, this might go on forever. It probably will. But if we cover it, you can pretend it's over. And what would you want to keep looking for, anyway? These are things none of us can really fathom. You'd just keep inventing alternatives to the word alternative, which itself is an alternative. An archive. An arrow pointing at our deepest fear for the day we feel ready to face it. That day may never come. That Messiah may never arrive to lift us up and out of the room with no windows or doors. The best we can hope for is a voice in the dark.

His feet touch ground. Blackout.

END OF PLAY

A Few Metaphilosophical Aphorisms
Matthew Gasda

1.   A philosophical diary tracks the de-subjectification of the subject. It is the journal of the subject on hunger-strike.

2.   Sight is destroyed by screens. Philosophy must grope forward blind.

3.   Philosophy must blind the screens which blind us.

4.   Marxism is dead as a historical truth or destiny. As a method of critique, it is more essential than ever.

5.   Philosophy is the tool the prey uses to track the progress of the hunter.

6.   Information is a toxin, knowledge is a cure.

7.   To be a subject is to be capable of willing subjectivity. Creative subjectivity.

8.   To philosophize is to learn to start over. Start anew. Dawn. Day after day.

9.   Everything has sped up except our concepts, which lag behind. Philosophy has not responded to the pressure (the present) of technology. Information, a function of capital, shapes culture like water shaping a landmass. The internet has carved a channel in the human; the topography of the

human has been permanently altered. If Christianity produced the first wave of the guilty consciousness, hyper-capitalism, or Information, produces the second wave: the guilt of not keeping up, not making enough money; of failing to maintain status in the digital realm. Philosophy, if it is to retain its practical power, must—can only—function as an inquiry and critique of this new and still evolving, or mutating, consciousness.

10.   A personal philosophy is a farmer's almanac of the mind. It tracks seasons, weather, yields. A first person philosophy turns the I against itself, the in-dividual into a -dividual. Constantly. Constant subjectivity. A hatred of objectification; an unwillingness to become a thing, to think like a thing; like a function, a machine-part. A personal philosophy is an antiseptic; cleanses the mind of its complicity with power—its desire to be one of, and with, the powerful. A personal philosophy founds itself on the subject, the subject which thinks it, the philosophy, into existence. A personal philosophy is the technology that cognition builds to save itself from other minds.

11.   Waking-life has become a fantasy; a corporate fantasy; a fantasy produced by advertising. The ethical subject, then, is the subject that is capable of dreaming. Dream life is the one domain of existence that has not been pierced through with advertising, with media. Dreams are not yet subject to the data revolution; to the power of the advertising algorithm. Only our dreams remain somewhat free.

12.   Philosophy is the coining of concepts, and to coin concepts, you must melt down words. The shell of language is familiar, the core is unfamiliar, alien. Take a word, break it open. This is a useful philosophical technique.

13.   Ordinary language—the highly cliched language of media-speak—is the ethical enemy; it is likewise reasonable to invoke other modes of speech, to try to rinse the thick crust of advertising rhetoric off of language.

14.   What worries me is that the short-term consequences of technology will be—are—nothing compared to the long-term consequences: the total erosion of cognitive silence, rest, stillness. Soon, we will no longer remember how to use the mental tools the mind builds to sharpen, deepen, and clarify itself: *the tools of inwardness.*